DARK OF NIGHT

A BURKE AND BLADE MYSTERY THRILLER
BOOK 4

MICHAEL LISTER

(John Jordan Novels)
<u>Power in the Blood</u>
<u>Blood of the Lamb</u>
<u>The Body and the Blood</u>
<u>Double Exposure</u>
<u>Blood Sacrifice</u>
<u>Rivers to Blood</u>
<u>Burnt Offerings</u>
<u>Innocent Blood</u>
<u>(Special Introduction by Michael Connelly)</u>
<u>Separation Anxiety</u>
Blood Money
Blood Moon
<u>Thunder Beach</u>
Blood Cries
<u>A Certain Retribution</u>
Blood Oath
Blood Work
Cold Blood
Blood Betrayal
Blood Shot
Blood Ties
Blood Stone
Blood Trail
Bloodshed
Blue Blood
And the Sea Became Blood
The Blood-Dimmed Tide
Blood and Sand
A John Jordan Christmas
Blood Lure

Blood Pathogen
Beneath a Blood-Red Sky
Out for Blood
What Child is This?
Blood Reckoning

(Burke and Blade Mystery Thrillers)
The Night Of
The Night in Question
All Night Long

(Jimmy Riley Novels)
The Girl Who Said Goodbye
The Girl in the Grave
The Girl at the End of the Long Dark Night
The Girl Who Cried Blood Tears
The Girl Who Blew Up the World

(Merrick McKnight / Reggie Summers Novels)
Thunder Beach
A Certain Retribution
Blood Oath
Blood Shot

(Remington James Novels)
Double Exposure
(includes intro by Michael Connelly)
Separation Anxiety
Blood Shot

(Sam Michaels / Daniel Davis Novels)
Burnt Offerings
Blood Oath
Cold Blood
Blood Shot

(Love Stories)
Carrie's Gift

(Short Story Collections)
North Florida Noir
Florida Heat Wave

Delta Blues
Another Quiet Night in Desperation

(The Meaning Series)
<u>Meaning Every Moment</u>
<u>The Meaning of Life in Movies</u>

Sign up for Michael's newsletter by clicking <u>here</u> or go to
www.MichaelLister.com and receive a free book.

For Denise
je t'aime beaucoup

SERIES SALE

For a limited time the entire John Jordan series is on sale!

CLICK HERE to complete your series for the best price EVER!

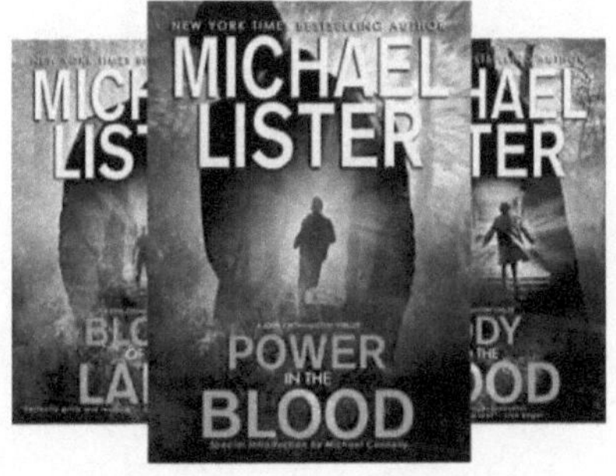

THE BURKE AND BLADE SERIES

Read the entire Burke and Blade Series.

Lucas Burke and Alix "Blade" Baker are Panama City Beach PIs specializing in missing persons cases--work they were led to by their own sister's disappearance.

Growing up in foster care and children's homes has made them tough, savvy, and streetwise, but nothing has prepared them for this.

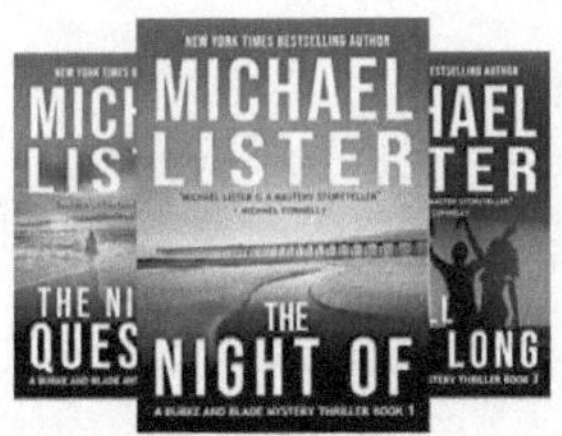

25 YEARS OF MICHAEL LISTER CRIME NOVELS

Local Author Celebrates 25 years of the John Jordan Mystery Series

Twenty-five years ago, when author Michael Lister was still the youngest chaplain with the Florida Department of Corrections, his first novel, "Power in the Blood," was being published. Now, twenty-five years later, Lister, who has been a full-time writer for the past twenty-two years, is publishing his 29th John Jordan mystery, "Blood Reckoning."

When asked about the inspiration for his crime novels, "Everything in my life is inspiration for my novels, but in terms of the specific inspirations for the nearly 30 John Jordan books, I've been inspired by actual true crime cases. I'm a true crime junkie and I find that the most fascinating unsolved cases eventually work their way into my books."

His new novel, "Blood Reckoning," while he's still grieving the loss of a close friend and co-worker, a young woman who has been like a daughter to him disappears.

Carla Pearson vanishes from a river camp cabin after her on-again-off-again boyfriend, Mason Hayes, leaves her there following an argument. The cabin is only accessible by boat and beyond it are thousands of acres of jungle-like swamps and dense, nearly impenetrable woods. What happened to Carla and who is responsible for her disappearance? Is it Mason Hayes? Is it her ex, Easton Stevens? His jealous wife? Or someone John hasn't even thought of?

John is in no condition to work this case but has no choice. He must find Carla before it's too late. He can't lose another loved one.

"I've written about John Jordan for twenty-eight years now," Lister said. "That's well over half my life. It has been so rewarding. John Jordan and I have gone through life together—and he's been an incredible and incredibly interesting compassion."

Publisher's Weekly calls Lister' work "Brilliantly conceived and executed. An impressive blend of procedural and fair-play whodunit. Lister expertly balances emotion and detection while doling out logical, gut-wrenching twists," and international bestseller Michael Connelly says "Michael Lister has become a mastery storyteller in his first 25 years and he's only getting started."

AUDIOBOOKS

MOST OF MICHAEL LISTER'S mystery thrillers are available on audiobook — and all will be soon.

CLICK HERE for more information and audiobook samples.

AUTHOR'S NOTE

Each book has a unique journey to publication. This one is no exception.

Parts of the book you're reading now were first written when I was figuring out what my next crime series would be. I had a few different ideas swirling around inside my head and so decided to write at least one of each in a potential new series to see what would happen. After writing my first Burke and Blade novel, I knew I wanted to write more, to spend more time with these characters, go on more adventures with them, and find out how their lives would unfold.

Once I was sure the Burke and Blade "Night" series was to become one of my main series, the question became what to do with the book I wrote as part of the other potential new series. And the answer I eventually arrived at was I would rewrite it as a Burke and Blade book.

So elements of *Dark of Night*, including the central mystery, were originally in a book titled *A Dark Radiant Rain*. If you happened to have read *A Dark Radiant Rain*, I think you'll find *Dark of Night* fascinating, not only because of how much new content is in it but also to compare how Burke and Blade investigate the case with how Sawyer Payne and Kace Mason did.

But whether *Dark of Night* is new to you or you've encountered some of it in *A Dark Radiant Rain*, I hope you thoroughly enjoy it and that it will leave you eagerly awaiting the next Burke and Blade mystery thriller. Because, Dear Reader, is also eagerly awaiting you.

PROLOGUE

IT WAS dark the night he disappeared. And raining.

A darkness deeper than mere darkness, a darkness more than night.

The rain was odd and soft and refracted the pale, anemic points of light scattered throughout the dark night in irregular and surreal ways, as if everything was taking place in a Dalí painting.

Dark sheets of mist in the night, hazy and hypnotic.

The band worked in all the songs about rain they knew, and by the end of their last set

had played CCR's "Have You Ever Seen the Rain," Prince's "Purple Rain," Dylan's "A Hard

Rain's A-Gonna Fall," Willie Nelson's "Blue Eyes Crying in the Rain," James Taylor's "Fire

and Rain," the Eurythmics' "Here Comes the Rain Again," and the Carpenters' "Rainy Days and

Mondays."

It was the kind of night that felt risky, unsteady, unsafe.

But there was nothing in the atypical atmosphere to portend a young man would so thoroughly and completely vanish off the face of the earth forever.

And yet, that's exactly what happened.

CHAPTER
ONE

LIKE EVERYONE, I am not just one thing but many.

My identity is derived from multiplicity.

I'm a man. I'm a musician. I am a finder of lost souls. I'm a friend, I'm a brother. I'm an uncle. I am rage. I am resilience.

But perhaps I am defined by what I am not even more than what I am.

I am not a son. I am not a member of a nuclear family.

What I am more than anything else is an orphan.

I hate the word. Loathe it. It sickens and angers me. But it also defines me.

I can still remember looking it up the first time I heard someone use it in connection with me.

The words are burned into my brain. Branded into my very flesh.

A child deprived by death of one or usually both parents. A young animal that has lost its mother. One deprived of some protection or advantage.

Many of us spend our lives asking who and what we are.

That's what I am. An orphan. Except it wasn't death that deprived me of parental protections and advantages and turned me into a young animal without a mother. My parents aren't dead. They're just dead to me. They didn't want me. Rejection not death orphaned me.

But to be an orphan is not only to be deprived of parents. It's to be deprived of any and all connection. It's to be utterly abandoned, completely alone.

I've spent my life alone.

But I've never felt as alone as I have since my foster sister Ashlynn took my niece Alana away from me.

The only person on the planet that I've ever been able to count on consistently is my partner and foster sister Blade, but we didn't really feel like a family until Ashlynn had Alana.

Ashlynn and Alana would often stay with me, and I'd keep Alana while her mom worked. And we formed an attachment unlike any I've ever had. And then she was taken away from me.

I can still remember what I felt when I woke to find this letter:

Dear Luc,

I'm sorry but I have to go. I have to get away from this place, from that man. I'm going to make a fresh start for me and Alana. Please understand. Please let us go. I've picked up a few tricks from you and Blade over the years and may be harder to find than you think, but I'm asking you, begging you, not to look for us. Please. Please let us go. This is what I want. This is what I need. Even if you find us I won't come back with you, so it would be a waste of time anyway. Thank you for all you've done. You have been such a great brother to me and a father figure and friend to Alana. I was wrong when I said we weren't family. You are about all the family we have in the world. I love you and I'll always be grateful to you for all you've done for me but especially for Alana. This isn't goodbye forever. We'll see you again one day. I promise.

Love always,

Ashlynn

CHAPTER
TWO

"MORNIN', Sunshine," Blade says as she walks into our office.

She is carrying two coffees and a box of doughnuts.

Since Ashlynn stole away in the night with Alana, Blade has been doing everything she can to cheer me up.

So far nothing has worked, but still she persists.

I appreciate the effort—especially since it so goes against her nature. She's not only my partner, but my person—the only person I have ever been able to count on consistently. On paper we're merely foster sibs who grew up in the system together, but we are far, far more than that. We're family—every bit as much as any blood relatives in the world.

Resembling a slightly undersized collegiate linebacker, she is wearing what I think of as her uniform—a pair of black ninja webbing drop-crotch multi-strap cargo pants, matte black greasy leather boots, a black retro leather biker jacket with lots of silver-toned zippers and a buckle belt at the bottom, a plain black tee, and small round dark shades beneath a black snapback hat worn backwards.

The only thing to change about her appearance in a very long time is her hair. It is now a series of short, rope-like dreads, half of which are in an up ponytail.

After handing me a coffee, she places the box of doughnuts on the desk and opens it.

"Why you in so early?" she asks, as she drops down into one of the client chairs and hooks her shades onto the band of her shirt.

We had just wrapped up a surveillance case and have nothing going at the moment.

I shrug.

The truth is I don't know. I'm just sort of lost. Have nothing else to do, so I came in early to think.

"We get a new case?" she asks.

I shake my head.

"Then it can only be one of two things," she says. "Which is it?"

"Which is what?"

"Your ass has been in here plotting," she says. "So which one you decide on? Takin' Dimitri off the board or trackin' down Ashlynn and Alana?"

Dimitri is a Russian mobster who had sworn to punch mine and Blade's tickets because of an altercation we had with him in which Blade cut up him and his bodyguard Bogdan. He has tried several times unsuccessfully. We have proven harder to take out than he thought we would be, and we have become an embarrassment to him. Recently, he discovered our connection to Ashlynn, who was working at one of his clubs, and vowed to kidnap and force both she and Alana to work in one of his brothels before killing us. He's the reason Ashlynn fled town with Alana.

Thinking of Dimitri trafficking Ashlynn and especially four-year-old Alana, makes me want to kill him with my bare hands —and take my time doing it. But wanting to do a thing and being able to do a thing are two different things.

Could I kill a man in cold blood?

I have anger issues and often lose myself in rage, and in that condition I am capable of almost anything, but to plot and plan and soberly extinguish a life . . . is a very different and deliberate act.

Even if I were morally and psychologically able to kill a monster like Dimitri, could I do so without getting killed myself? Could I do it without getting caught?

The other option Blade asked about—tracking down Ashlynn and Alana—which I have been tempted to do even though she begged me not to, wouldn't solve the ultimate problem. Knowing they are well and safe would make me less anxious and seeing them again would make me less lonely. But it would do nothing toward fixing the Dimitri problem.

"There's a third option," I say.

"Oh, yeah. What's that?"

I remove the lid from my coffee cup and blow into it and feel the rising steam on my face.

"The one I've been choosing so far," I say. "I can keep doing nothing."

"Thinkin' through everything, plotting, tryin' to figure out how to do it ain't nothin'," she says.

"True."

"You know we can figure out how to do it," she says. "And we can pull it off without gettin' caught."

"I'm not as convinced as you are of either of those," I say. "But it's getting the first one right that really matters. I don't want to get caught, but if that's what it costs, Ashlynn and Alana are worth it. If we decide to do it I just want to make sure we can actually do it. It won't be easy. He's nearly always surrounded by a lot of bodyguards and firepower. It's not just Bogdan now that he's taken over for Lev."

Lev Sokolov, Dimitri's uncle, was recently killed—some suspect by Dimitri—and now Dimitri is in charge.

"Maybe so, but if Lev could be taken out, Dimitri can."

"Lev was taken out by someone close to him," I say. "Had to be. How we gonna get close enough to Dimitri to do it?"

"You got to figure out *if* you want to do it first," she says. "Then we'll figure out *how*."

"I'm not there yet."

She nods. "Be sure to let me know when you are. And if any of us are still alive by then we'll do something about it."

I sip some coffee and eat a doughnut.

The doughnuts are still warm and soft and the glaze sticks to my fingers.

"I've been thinking," I say.

"I know," she says. "That's what we've been talkin' about."

"Why don't we work Kaylee's case," I say. "I mean really reinvestigate it. Not the way we've been doing it—a little here, a little there, in between other things. We've got nothing going right now."

"That thing about an attorney who represents himself has a fool for a client," she says. "That apply to PIs?"

I nod. "Definitely."

"You're sayin' work it just like one of our other cases."

"Yeah. We've gotten better. Have a ton more experience now. We'd still have fools for clients, but . . ."

Kaylee Walsh, our foster sister, went missing when she was twenty-one and we were kids. Her disappearance hangs over us, haunts us. It's the reason we became finders of lost souls.

When Kaylee was just a junior at the University of Florida in Gainesville, for reasons no one has ever discovered, she lied to her professors about a family emergency and left campus without telling anyone. Later that night, on a flat stretch of rural road in Georgia, she ran off the highway into a ditch. Then, even with witnesses watching from a nearby farmhouse, in the span of some six minutes, she disappeared off the face of the earth. Vanished into thin air. Without a trace. Never to be seen again. That was ten long years ago, and we're no closer to finding her now than when she first went missing.

"Lexi gonna let you leave?" she asks. "We'd have to go to Gainesville and South Georgia."

Lexi Miller is my probation officer. I have two years of probation remaining on my sentence, during which time I'm not allowed to leave Panama City.

Lexi can give me permission to travel within the state, but an out of state travel pass would have to be approved by her supervisor.

"I can ask," I say. "Since it's work I might be able to get a—"

"Ain't talkin' about as your probation officer," she says with a smile. "Meant 'cause she'll miss your ass too much."

Lexi is also one of two women I've been seeing some. It's complicated, and, in the case of Lexi, against all the rules. If it goes tits up it could cost me my freedom and her her job.

"What about the Mom?" she adds. "Can she do without you for a few days?"

The Mom is how Blade refers to Heather Harrison, the other woman I've been seeing—not only because she was the mother of a missing child in a case we worked but because she is nearly old enough to be my mother.

"Tell you what," I say. "Let's take a turn talkin' about your love life for a while."

CHAPTER
THREE

I MEET Lexi for lunch at Mosey's.

Mosey's is a bar, restaurant, and live music venue in the old Mini Mall building on Grace Avenue in downtown Panama City.

We are in the back booth in the side room which affords us a modicum of privacy.

It's mid afternoon on a weekday and we've virtually got the place to ourselves, unlike this past weekend, when we were here for the Misfit Market—an eclectic, artistic gathering of vendors offering the coolest, oddest, weirdest collections of vinyl, vintage clothes, books, baked goods, original art, jewelry, and even taxidermy.

I'm having a slice of the Great White and she's having a salad.

"How are you?" she asks.

She is a petite blond with Gulf-green eyes, a pale, simple face, and the body of a runner. Her thickish hair, which was up when she arrived, is now down, and the ends touching the tips of her shoulders are still damp.

"I'm okay," I say. "I'm happy to be sitting across from you."

"Care to elaborate?"

"Well, I enjoy your company and I like the looks of you and—"

"I meant about you just being okay."

I smile. I knew what she meant.

"I miss Alana. I'm worried about her and Ashlynn. I don't know what to do about Dimitri. I'm sick of being Logan's lapdog and having the threat of going back to prison hanging over me, and I feel bad about Brooklyn Hill."

"Thank you," she says. "I appreciate you letting me in a little."

"How are *you*?" I ask.

She gives a little shrug. "I'm okay. Worried about you."

"Don't waste time doing that," I say. "I'm okay. I'll be okay. Just have to figure out how to protect Alana."

"I'm worried about us, too," she says. "I think I thought we were something we're not . . . or . . . I don't know. You seem like you . . . like maybe you're not as into me as you were." She shakes her head. "That sounds so juvenile, but I'm not sure how else to say it. I know we're—that what we can be is limited until you come off probation, and I know I fucked up, but . . . even given all that. It just seems you've cooled on me. It's like we're more casual and . . . I don't know . . . less intense than we were."

Logan Owens, the so called victim of my crime, and the reason I did time and am now on probation, is blackmailing us—me more than her so far—but when she first received the incriminating photos, she thought I was behind them and showed up at my door with armed muscle.

"I understand," I say, "and I'm sorry. But given all that is going on with Alana and Ashlynn, Dimitri and Logan—not to mention the risks we're taking just to do what we're doing—I don't see how we can be anything more than what we are right now. The truth is I don't have any more to give. And I understand if that's not enough and you want or need to stop altogether."

"I'm not there yet," she says. "I'm not, but . . . this whole thing is so fucked."

"Yes, it is."

The main room of Mosey's is a large, open space with a tile floor and nothing but hard surfaces, and every noise from out there echoes through the place—someone opening and closing a door, walking across the floor, throwing a bottle into a trash can full of them.

"I see two nuclear options," she says. "We could stop seeing each other—except professionally or . . . I could quit my job and we could be together."

"But you're not there yet—for either one of them—right?"

"Right."

"I need to ask a favor," I say. "I'd like to go away a few days to work Kaylee's case. We could both spend that time thinking about what we want to do next."

She looks up and nods slowly as if considering it. "I think that could be a good thing. I'll cover for you on this end, but if you get caught . . ."

"You knew nothing about it," I say.

"You've got to be super careful," she says. "You can't get so much as a speeding ticket or you'll be going back to prison."

CHAPTER
FOUR

AS I'M CROSSING Grace heading toward the parking lot behind the Martin Theater, my phone rings.

It's not a number I recognize but I answer it anyway.

The afternoon sun is hidden behind a wall of clouds and the day is gray, the colors of the landscape below drained, desaturated.

"Burke," I say.

"Hey, Luc," Alana says.

In that moment, with those two words, the world entire becomes a lighter, better, more beautiful place, and it seems as though the clouds part and the sun shines through, though it does not.

"*Hey, Alana,*" I say, my voice full of the joy and relief I feel. "How are you?"

"I miss you," she says.

Her little voice is low and has a slight hoarse quality to it.

"I miss you so much. Are you and your mommy okay?"

"Yeah. I'm bored. I want you to keep me, not smelly old Mrs. Fritos Feet."

A loud burst of laughter flies out of my mouth.

"Mommy wants to talk to you," she says.

"Wait," I say.

"Yeah?"

"What have you been doing? What have you been watching? Playing?"

"Nobody plays with me like you do," she says. "Been watchin' Huggy Wuggy. He doesn't scare me anymore. And Sonic and Cookie World C."

She means the Youtube Channel CookieSwirlC.

"I'm glad Huggy Wuggy doesn't scare you anymore. I sure miss watching videos with you and playing."

"Mom's always tired and Old Mrs. Fritos Feet doesn't know how to pretend stuff."

"Have you been taking your princess pill, drinking water, and brushing your teeth?"

"No."

Princess pills are what we call her daily multi-vitamins.

"Why not?"

"*I don't know,*" she says, her voice rising in a way that makes me miss her even more. "Here's Mama."

"I love you so much," I say. "And I miss you. Hope to see you soon."

"Love you, *bye,*" she says and is gone.

"Hey, Luc," Ashlynn says.

"Thank you so much for letting me talk to her. How are you?"

"Okay. Miss you and Blade and the gang. Miss Panama City more than I ever thought I would."

I'm standing on the sidewalk on the east side of Grace. It's quiet and there's very little traffic—only the occasional passing pedestrian and vehicle.

"Are y'all safe? Doing well?"

"Have you tried to find us?" she asks.

"I've wanted to every single second of every single day," I say. "But so far I've resisted."

"That means more to me than you can ever know," she says.

"Respecting my wishes. Giving me space and freedom. I've always known you'd do anything you could for us but I didn't think you'd . . . let us go."

"It has been harder than you can imagine."

"Makes me trust you even more."

"I miss y'all," I say. "Miss taking care of Alana . . . but more than anything else I just want y'all to be safe and well."

"I know. And we are—ish. Alana misses you so much . . . and no one takes care of her like you do—not even me."

"I have a big Alana shaped hole right in the middle of me," I say.

"Do you think you could come here without anyone knowing or following you?"

"Absolutely."

"If you can . . . I've got a mystery for you to solve, but if you can't . . . I don't want Dimitri following you here and killing us."

"I won't let that happen," I say. "I swear."

"SO, WAIT," Blade says. "You got permission to leave town so we could reinvestigate Kaylee's case, but instead we going to see Ashlynn and Alana and work a case for her."

"Not for her, per se, but one she thinks we should investigate."

She starts to say something, but I add, "We'd be going to check on them. We can look into the case or not. That's almost irrelevant."

"And Kaylee?" she asks.

"We'll re-investigate hers from top to bottom next chance we get," I say. "You know I want to, but . . . I can't miss this opportunity to see Alana and check on them. I can go alone if you prefer."

"Oh, so I ask a few questions and suddenly my black ass is uninvited."

I laugh. "We've got to make sure we're not followed," I say. "Leave everything here—including our phones and devices. Borrow a vehicle. Only use burner phones and cash. Can't take a chance on leading Dimitri to them."

"We could do all that," she says, "or . . . we could just drop by and shoot Dimitri in the face on our way out of town."

I laugh again. "Tempting."

She says, "So where are they and what's the case"

"Forgotten Coast Estates."

"The retirement place?

The Estates is a massive coastal retirement community, nearly a city unto itself, less than fifty miles east of here.

Blade says, "She didn't run far, did she?"

"They're living with and helping care for a woman who was recently widowed—and Ashlynn is working at a bar in the nearby town of Bridgeport."

"So what's the case?"

"A guy walks into a bar," I say. "Stop me if you've heard this one before."

"Let me guess," she says. "He walked in and never walked out—just like Brooklyn Hill, which is what made her think of us."

"Exactly," I say. "Every entrance and exit are covered by cameras. They capture him walking in, but he never walks out."

Aiden Shaw, a 27-year-old medical student, was at the Estates visiting his parents at Halloween two years ago. After begrudgingly helping his dad hand out candy to all the eager little trick-or-treaters so that his mom could attend an out-of-town party with her best friend, he went on a costumed pub-crawl with his on-again off-again friend Brad Reed.

After several hours and far more shots, the two wound up at Psycho Suzi's, a trying-to-be trendy bar a couple of blocks outside the Estates. Somewhere along the way, Brad had met up with Jade Oborne, a sometime girlfriend, who accompanied them to Psycho Suzi's.

Psycho Suzi's is on the second story of an entertainment complex, part of which was under construction at the time. The three are shown riding up the escalator to the bar at 1:15 a.m. Later, at 1:50 a.m., the same camera shows Aiden standing out in front of the bar on the landing near the escalator talking to two young women. After a few moments, he steps out of frame and back into the bar.

Aiden Shaw is never seen again.

Security cameras cover every entrance and exit of the building. Aiden is clearly shown entering the bar, but never exiting.

Brad and Jade, who can be seen leaving via the escalator at 2:01 a.m., claim they both searched for and called Aiden before leaving, but unable to find him and getting no answer, assumed he had left without them. Not only is that something he had done before, but he and Brad had engaged in a drunken argument earlier and had split up sometime around 1:30 a.m.

The two young men had never been especially close, and it seems as if nearly every encounter ended in an argument, but for some reason they had continued to hang out occasionally over the years.

Not only had Brad peppered his early statements to the police and media with subtle and not so subtle criticisms of Aiden, but he quickly lawyered up and refused to take a polygraph—the only person asked by authorities to do so.

CHAPTER
SIX

"*LUC*," Alana squeals as she runs toward me.

I let her momentum carry her forward and lift her up and spin her around.

Then I pull her to me and hug her as tight as I dare.

I've missed you so much," I say.

Blade says, "*BLADE*" in a playful mimic of what Alana just did.

Ashlynn says, "Say hey to your Aunt Blade."

"Hey, Aunt Blade."

"It's so good to see y'all," Ashlynn says.

"Good to see you, runaway," Blade says.

"Sorry about that," she says. "I panicked. Are y'all sure you weren't followed."

"Positive," Blade says. "No one would ever believe my black ass would come to a place like this."

She shakes her head as she looks around at all the little boxes made of ticky tacky that make up the homogenized Estates neighborhood.

"Got to be the whitest place on earth," she says.

"Come to the backyard and I'll introduce you to Ms. Sheri."

"I need a hug from this little girl first," Blade says.

"Can't let her go yet," I say.

"I'll give her right back, damn."

I hand Alana over and she and Blade hug. As they do, I step over and embrace Ashlynn.

"I'm so happy to see you," I say. "So glad y'all are okay."

She nods. "We're good. Just miss y'all."

"This is Sheri Shaw," Ashlynn is saying.

We are in Sheri's lush flower garden behind her house, which, like most homes in the Estates, borders a manicured golf course.

The October afternoon sun slants in at an angle, the only object in the clear blue sky. It's warm, but not hot, and the humidity level has dropped to a more pleasing percentage.

Like many of the homes in the Estates, Sheri's postage stamp lot backs up to the fairway of one of the many holes of the excessive golf courses that weave in and out and around and through every other element of the Estates.

The Estates-provided barrier between Sheri's few feet of yard and the golf course is made up of planted palms, flowering shrubs, perennials, and annuals that follow the curve of the sand traps on this side. But the real barrier is Sheri's elaborate and verdant flower garden—something that violates the strict Estates covenants and is under constant threat of being forcibly removed.

I am holding Alana again, who seems to have grown a foot in the short time since I had seen her. Ashlynn and Blade are on either side of us.

I can't imagine ever letting go of Alana again—and she doesn't seem to want me to.

"It's very nice to meet you both," Sheri says.

Sheri is an older woman who doesn't look her age. She is trim and fit and has a youthful bearing. Beneath her modern, stylish, short blond hair, her pampered face shows only the finest lines and slightest looseness of skin.

You can tell that Blade makes her uncomfortable—mostly by the way she tries to act like she doesn't.

"Y'all are most welcome here," Sheri says. "Most welcome. These two have missed y'all terribly. I'm so glad y'all've come to see them."

"Thank you," I say. "We've missed them more than we can say."

"Tell them about your break-in," Ashlynn says. "They can help. They're very good at this sort of thing."

Sheri nods toward the back of her house.

I turn and follow her gaze. Beyond the little outdoor table holding a few ficus plants, one side of the white French doors is boarded up, its jam splintered, the striker plate hanging down, small shards of glass still on the patio.

"It's coming up on the two-year anniversary of my son's disappearance," she says. "Someone broke into my house pretending to be him."

"You sure it wasn't him?" Blade asks.

Sheri nods. "Mothers have special connections to their children. It wasn't him. I'm not sayin' it couldn't be—I'd know if Aiden were dead. I'd feel it in my womb. And he's not. He's still out there somewhere. And I'd have known if it were him that night—even with him whispering in the dark with a mask on."

I'm not so sure about the connection between mothers and children—and not just because I've never experienced it. I've known many mothers who were convinced their children were still alive right up until their dead bodies were discovered.

"This should be the safest place on earth," Ashlynn says.

The Estates are marketed as the safest community in Florida, and it's a big part of the attraction to retirees who flock here—particularly the divorced and widowed women who live alone.

"Still can't believe it happened here," Ashlynn adds. "Who would do such a thing?"

"You know what I think," Sheri says.

Ashlynn nods. "She's being pressured to move."

"Something I'm not going to do," Sheri says. "I've got to be here for when Aiden really comes home."

"The Estates want to expand the golf course to be eligible for certain PGA Tour Events," Ashlynn says. "They're offering her more than her home is worth and they're saying she doesn't have to move far, but . . ."

"I'm not going anywhere," Sheri says.

"She's been through so much," Ashlynn says. "Too much. They need to leave her alone. Poor thing."

Blade says, "It could be whoever signed the online funeral guestbook."

Sheri looks up at her surprised. "So you know about that."

I say, "Ashlynn told us about Aiden's disappearance, so we read up on the case on the way here."

Less than two short months after Aiden vanished, his dad, Philip, had fallen from the attic while retrieving Christmas decorations. Crashing through insulation and the ceiling to land on the hallway floor, he had seemed fine at the time—just bruised and sore once the wind that had been knocked out of him returned. But three days later he died suddenly of a delayed aortic dissection—the trauma from the fall causing a small tear in his aorta that went undetected. His injury caused no real pain or cause for concern, and then without warning his injured aorta gave way and ruptured.

The funeral home providing his burial services had an online guestbook for friends and family to sign who couldn't attend the memorial service. One of the entries read: Miss you, Dad. See you soon. Love, your son, Aiden (the Virgin Islands).

Blade says, "Bastard capable of that kind of cruelty could certainly break in and—what exactly did he do?"

"I'm not convinced it wasn't Aiden who signed the book," Sheri says. "I know what the cops say, but . . . just because he wasn't really in the Virgin Islands doesn't mean it wasn't him. But I know for a fact that guy tonight wasn't."

She's right. Just because the authorities discovered that the IP address used to send the message to the virtual guestbook was a local internet cafe and not somewhere in the Virgin Islands doesn't mean it wasn't Aiden. If he really did walk out of his life like some theorize, he'd pick a place as far away as he could to sign in from. It was odd to include a place in parentheses like that anyway. No one else did.

"As far as what he did when he broke in . . ." Sheri says. "When I woke up he was holding me down—sitting on my stomach, pinning my arms to the bed. He was wearing a mask and a costume of some sort. Told me not to be afraid, he wasn't here to hurt me, but . . . Said he was my Aiden, but I know it wasn't. Aiden would never do something like that to me. He knows I have a weak heart. He was whispering. Hard to hear and understand, but . . . the way he called me Mom . . . It wasn't him. I just know it. Said he was healthy and happy and to stop looking for him. Just let him live his life in the peace it took him so long to find. And then there was a noise outside—have no idea what it was. It scared him. He took off. Crashed through my back door and disappeared on the golf course. Didn't hurt me—well, besides my wrists a little."

She rubs her right wrist with her left hand, then rubs her left wrist with her right hand.

"Did he take anything?" I ask.

"Not that I know of," she says. "I have't noticed anything missing."

"He have a weapon?" Blade asks.

"Not that I saw."

"What kind of mask was it?" I ask.

She shakes her head. "I'm not sure. It was dark. And to be honest I had my eyes closed much of the time."

"You remember how he smelled or anything else about him?"

Her eyes widen. "Oh, wow, he did have a peculiar smell . . . Kind of . . . rubbery."

"Could it have been latex?" I say. "Like a Halloween mask."

Her eyes widen again, accompanied by her mouth opening this time, and she begins to nod—slowly at first. "Yes," she says. "That's it. Aiden went missing on Halloween."

CHAPTER
SEVEN

SINCE THE BREAK-IN, Sheri, Ashlynn, and Alana have been staying across the street with Robin, a friend of Sheri's. While Sheri, Ashlynn, and Alana go over to get their things, Blade and I take a look around the crime scene.

There's no crime scene tape or any sign of an investigation at Sheri place, and Ashlynn has told us there hadn't been even from the beginning. Homes don't get broken into in the Estates. It doesn't fit the narrative of the safest community in Florida.

"Okay," Blade says, "She wakes up with him on top of her in the middle of the night. There's no sign of forced entry. He whispers that shit about being her son and wanting to be left alone and then he hears a noise, gets spooked, and takes off, crashing through the patio doors, and disappearing on the golf course. She calls for help—You think Estates Security or Golf Force or whatever they called even reported it to the sheriff's department?" Blade asks.

"Golf Force," I say with an appreciative laugh. "Nice. I doubt it."

We start with the broken back door.

The door on the right appears to be untouched, undamaged. The one on the left, the boarded-up one, is splintered above and below the handle mechanism, its inside face near the tempered glass bearing a partial boot print, presumably from where the assailant kicked the door open on his way out.

We examine the hardware, hinges, and lock stile.

"Wouldn't take much force to kick it open," I say.

"She countin' on the Estates not her doors and locks to protect her."

"Probably not anymore."

We enter the small house and begin looking around.

It's immaculate. Everything is in its place and every place is pristine clean.

"Smells good as shit up in here," Blade says. "What's that smell?"

"Money," I say.

"My money never smell like this."

"You have to have a certain amount and have had it for a certain amount of time for it to smell like this."

The feminine furniture appears new, and it's obviously expensive without being extravagant. The walls and tabletops are peppered with framed photographs of Aiden and his father, but there are very few pictures of the three of them.

Sheri lost her only child and her husband within two months two years ago. She became a widow and an—Not an orphan. What is the name for a parent who loses a child?

I can't come up with anything and conclude there isn't a name—probably because such an experience shouldn't exist to need a name.

The floor plan of the little home is a master suite on one side, two bedrooms with a Jack and Jill bathroom between them on the other, and an open-concept living room, dining room, and kitchen between them.

When they built, Phil and Sheri added a few features to customize their particular little box, but none more elaborate and dramatic than the white stone fireplace. They probably have to run the air-conditioning in order to use it even a few times a year, but it would be worth it. It, like nearly every other surface of the house, is decorated with pictures of Aiden, including one in a Halloween costume from his last night. It was snapped in front of the house as he and his dad passed out candy, but Sheri has folded it so that Phil is cropped out. As with some of the other photos, it is strategically placed to cover flaws and deep gouges in the unique stone.

We cross the little living room and open the first of the two doors to find a standard if overly furnished guest room.

Turning and opening the other door directly behind me, I find a shrine of sorts to Aiden in the room that presumably has been left much as it was the last time he stayed in it—only now with the addition of items from his dorm room.

"It's funny," Blade says. "We know what it's like to be on the other side of this—losing parents—but I have no idea and I never will what it's like to lose a child."

"I got a glimpse of it when we lost Alana," I say.

"Yeah, I guess," she says. "You got a connection with her I don't have. Hell, you got a connection with her I'm not capable of having."

Making our way between the dining room table and kitchen island, we stop at the entryway to the master suite and examine the door.

It bears no marks of violence, no signs of forced entry.

"Wonder if it was locked?" I say.

"May not have even been closed."

Stepping into the bedroom, I walk over and check the bedroom and bathroom windows.

Finding them securely fastened with no signs of damage, I say, "We know how the guy got out, but we have no idea how he got in."

We walk out of the suite, past the kitchen, and down a little hallway to the front door. We study the door connecting the two-car garage, then move past the burgundy Honda Pilot to the garage door itself.

"No sign of break-in," Blade says. "Only breakout."

"If he has a key that would narrow it down considerably."

Blade says, "Coulda been somebody she knows. They drop by for a little social visit and unlock a door or window while they was here. Or he coulda come on an official visit—a maintenance or repair person of some kind—and done the same thing."

"Maybe he broke in the backdoor but breaking out of it covered the evidence up."

She shrugs. "It's possible. We should take another look at the door. "Remember the other break-in?"

Approximately two months after Aiden went missing and just after her husband's death, Sheri's house was broken into. The investigation conducted by both the Estates security and the Creek County Sheriff's Department concluded that the break-in was unrelated to Aiden's disappearance. It was the holidays and there were a string of burglaries in the wider area, and it appeared that only a few presents and electronics were taken from her home. Sheri's place was the only one in her neighborhood hit by the thieves, which made the authorities take a closer look at it than they might otherwise have, but ultimately they determined that she may have been targeted because she was a single older woman whose son had vanished and whose husband had recently died in a tragic accident.

"Coulda been connected to Aiden's disappearance after all" she says. "Whoever it was coulda commandeered a spare key while he was here?"

"We need to ask Sheri if all her keys are accounted for."

"There's also the possibility that it actually *was* Aiden," she says. "His ass has a key."

"True. But if he had a key or a way in of some sort . . . why not use it on his way out?"

She shrugs. "His ass was in a hurry. Or wanted to escape through the golf course. Or wanted everyone to think he didn't have a key."

I start to say something, but golf course maintenance men working on the sand trap catch my eye.

"There's a good chance he ran through there as he was making his escape."

"Then we should go see what they up to," she says.

"We certainly should."

We make our way through Sheri's garden and backyard and toward the golf course.

"Whitest fuckin' game in the world," Blade says.

"I don't know," I say. "Curling might have something to say about that."

As we approach the sand trap, we see that the two men in the green Estates sports shirts and khaki shorts are digging something out of it.

We reach them in time to see one of them hold up a black Halloween costume with the small sand trap rake.

It's a black robe with a hood and cape, a dusting of pure white sand covering it.

As the other one reaches down for the mask, I say, "Wait. Don't touch it."

"Huh?"

"There was a break-in a few nights ago in the house over there. I think this is what the guy was wearing."

"*Really?*" the one leaning over the mask says, and they both begin to look at the items with awe and appreciation.

"We need to call the Creek County Sheriff's Department and have them come out for it."

"We have to call Estates security," the one holding the costume with the rake says. "They call the sheriff."

"Okay," I say. "Let's snap some pictures and be sure not to touch anything."

Without waiting for them to respond, I step forward and begin to take pictures of the items.

The mask is that of a plain, white, expressionless face, disturbing because of its emptiness, creepy in its inhumanity.

CHAPTER
EIGHT

"WE APPRECIATE YOU CALLING US," Rick Carson is saying.

He's an investigator with the Creek County Sheriff's Department, and he's sitting in Sheri's living room with me, Blade, Sheri, Ashlynn, and Robin. Alana is playing in her room.

Even in the middle of a random weekday afternoon, Robin Shepherd looks regal—a result of both her bearing and her beauty and her pampered, monied lifestyle. She has dark, shortish hair that doesn't appear dyed, and dark, penetrating eyes, the lids of which don't sag down to obscure them.

After taking pictures of the costume, we had called the sheriff's department, not sure that the Estates security would.

"You'd be surprised at how often incidents and even crimes happen here in the Estates aren't reported to us," Rick says.

He's a youngish, thickish white man with short, side-parted blondish hair and a gentleness not often associated with law enforcement.

"Were y'all notified of the break-in here a few nights ago?" I ask.

"That's a perfect example," he says. "We weren't."

While we're talking, Robin had gotten up and slipped into the kitchen.

"That's . . ." Sheri says, "outrageous."

"The Estates is a very safe place to live," Rick says, "but those who own and operate it are trying to sell the notion that it's the safest place on the planet, so they tend to try to suppress anything that contradicts that."

"Which makes it less not more safe," I say.

"You're absolutely right about that," Rick says. "It's true that most of the time it's related to theft and drunk and disorderly, but occasionally it's related to very serious crimes like assault, rape, maybe even murder."

Sheri shakes her head and lets out a long, heavy sigh.

Robin joins us again, a tray with glasses of iced tea and a plate of store-bought shortbread cookies on it in her hands. She sets it down on the coffee table between us.

We thank her and each take a glass. Rick Carson is the only one to take a cookie. And he takes three.

"You mind taking me through what happened the other night?" Rick asks Sheri around a crunchy, crumbly bite of his cookie.

"I was sound asleep and suddenly someone was on top of me, pressing me down, pinning my arms to the bed, covering my mouth. It was very dim, but the nightlight in the bathroom kept it from being pitch black. He had on a mask."

"Like this one?" I ask, holding up my phone to show her the picture of the mask found in the sand trap.

"I'll need to get those from you," Rick says.

Sheri nods. "Yes. I think so. I closed my eyes and . . . I was so scared. He whispered some stuff. It was hard to hear. I didn't make out some of it. But it was something like 'Mom, it's me. I'm okay. I just wanted you to know not to worry about me.' Some other stuff I didn't understand. 'I'm playing in a band. I'm happy. Please don't look for me anymore. I'll be in touch.' There was a banging on the front door and he was gone."

"Do you believe it was your son?" Rick asks.

Sheri is shaking her head before he finishes the question. "I know it wasn't. A mother knows. I know he's still alive, but that wasn't him."

"Did he have any distinguishing . . . *anything*?" Rick asks. "Smells, mannerisms, ticks, accent, speech patterns, movements? Anything."

"No," she says. "At least I don't think so. I really didn't . . . My eyes were closed. I was so scared. I'm afraid I'm a terrible witness."

"Not at all," Rick says.

"Do you mind if I ask . . ." I say, looking from Rick to Sheri. "Any idea how he got in?"

She looks confused. "Broke in the back patio door."

"Actually, that's where he broke out," I say, and explain to them what Blade and I discovered and theorized about the assailant's entry into and exit from the house.

"That's very interesting," Rick says. "I'll have to take a look at that. I'm familiar with y'all, by the way. Read online about some of the missing persons cases y'all solved in Panama City Beach. Some very impressive work."

"Thank you," I say.

"I just assumed he broke in," Sheri continues. "If he didn't . . . I have no idea how he—"

"Anyone been in recently to do any work for you or repair anything?" I ask.

She thinks about it, then shakes her head. "Don't think so."

"Who all has a key?" Blade asks.

If Rick minds us asking questions he doesn't show it.

"No one that would do anything like that," she says.

Rick says, "I'm sure not, but we need to check with them. Make sure they still have them."

"I'd have to think about it," she says. "I can make you a list. A couple of neighbors for when I go on vacation." She turns toward Robin. "Robin has one and . . . Ah . . . Let's see who else .

. . My cleaning lady. Aiden has one, of course. And Amanda. A few others. I'll—"

"Aiden's ex-girlfriend Amanda?" Rick asks.

"I assume she still has one," she says. "I never got it back from her. And she's not his ex."

"Didn't she get engaged recently?"

"Well, yes, but I just . . . Only because she believes Aiden is dead. But I just meant . . . They didn't break up."

"Okay," Rick says. "Sure, I . . . I know what you mean. But yes, if you could make me a list of everyone who has ever had a key . . ."

"I'll do it today . . . as long as you promise not to harass them."

"I promise, ma'am," he says. "That's not how I— That's not my style."

"I have to say this," she says. "I was scared. It was a frightening experience, but . . . I was never in any real danger. Whoever it was didn't intend me any harm. I could tell."

"I APPRECIATE YOU CALLING ME," Rick Carson is saying, "more than you know. And the pictures of the costume and mask are . . . they help a lot. I realize the . . . Aiden's disappearance took place outside of the Estates . . . but *just* outside. And Aiden was staying here. As were Brad and Jade, so there's an obvious connection even if it's not direct, but the Estates won't cooperate. Who knows, we may have had this thing solved already if they would just assist us—or at least not obstruct us."

Blade, Rick, and I are standing out in Sheri's small yard in the early afternoon.

"I'm so . . . It's . . . This case is baffling enough without them handicapping me. Two years and not so much as a single solid clue. The media acts like we don't care or that we're just bumbling idiots, but . . . you can't imagine the pressure I feel. Nobody—except Aiden's mom—wants to find him more than I do."

I say, "It's obvious you care very deeply."

"I do," he says. "I feel so bad for Mrs. Shaw and poor Amanda. I know people say she moved on awfully fast, but I saw how heartbroken she was. She was so in love with him. I think she was expecting to get proposed to on their vacation that next week. Anyway . . . I'm not too proud to ask for help. That insight y'all had about the break-in . . . that was good. I don't know how long y'all will be visiting, but I'd appreciate any help you'd be willing to give on this case. Like I said I've been impressed by the work you've done, and it'd really help having someone here inside the Estates. You would be able to get so much more information than I would. You'll hear things. See things. Make connections. Be able to ask questions. It would have to be just between us. My boss would never go for anything like this, but if you're willing . . . I'll take all the help I can get. I only care about clearing the case and I'm more than happy for civilians to help get that done. But . . . I'm in the minority in that view."

"We'd be happy to," I say.

"Just need to keep it super secretive."

Blade says, "So don't blab about it on social media?"

"We'll keep it quiet."

"Thing is . . . more and more I'm being pulled off this case for other more immediate ones. It's not getting the attention I want to give it, and my supervisor's not amenable to my requests to spend more time on it. I could really use some help and I think you'd be great."

"When could you bring us up to speed on Aiden's disappearance?" I ask. "Let us in on the details only y'all know?"

"Probably be best to talk about it while doing a walkthrough of Suzi's, but . . . essentially all entrances and exits were covered by cameras. Aiden can be seen walking in with Brad Reed and Jade Oborne and he can be seen a little before closing time talking to two girls out front, but as they leave he heads back into the bar, and he is never seen leaving. We searched every inch of that bar and the building it's in. We watched every second of all the video footage from that night—over and over again. We got the surveillance footage from all the nearby businesses. We've looked at all of it. He's not on any of it. It's the most . . . He went into the bar. We know that. He never came out of the bar. We know that. He's not still in the bar. We know that. That's all we know. We haven't gotten anywhere really. There are all sorts of wild theories and crazy speculation online, and we get bizarre tips but it's all garbage—just bored people playing cyber Sherlock. I know people are frustrated with us," Rick says. "But there's only one case like this in the history of missing persons. *One*. It's the most baffling missing persons case ever. And it's not unsolved for lack of effort. I've worked my ass off on it. And not just me. And I know we're a small department, but we've had investigators from several other agencies consult on this. It's on me because it's my case, but the best and brightest haven't been able to solve it either."

The front door opens and Robin walks out.

It's obvious she's walking home, but she veers off to speak to us.

CHAPTER
TEN

"I'M REALLY WORRIED ABOUT SHERI," she says. "I think she should stay with me until y'all can figure out what's going on. But she keeps saying what if she was wrong and it *was* Aiden who broke in. She says she wants to be here for when he comes back—or comes for the first time if that wasn't him. It's why she won't sell her house even though they're offering her a fortune. She's not eating right. Not sleeping. Just obsessed with staying in her home waiting for Aiden's return. But he's not coming home, is he?"

It's common for families of the missing to refuse to move or change anything—their address, their phone numbers, anything —as a desperate act of faith that their loved one might just return to them one day.

According to Ashlynn, a lot of the residents of the Estates believe that even though the Estates needs Sheri's property for the course expansion, they're also keen to get rid of her garden and, ultimately, remove the house that's associated with such a dark and tragic event—the kind that isn't allowed to happen to residents of the Estates.

"A lot of people think he just took off," Robin continues, "that he decided to start a new life somewhere else."

"There are people who say that about nearly every missing person," I say. "And they want to believe it, but vanishing without a trace is nearly impossible. Especially these days. Especially when so many people are searching for you. It takes a ton of money and a world-class new identity, and there's no evidence he had either. It takes precision and precise planning. It's not something you do impulsively after a night of heavy drinking."

Robin nods and thinks about it. "But . . ." she says, "nearly impossible is not the same as impossible. And none of the possible scenarios seem possible, do they? The whole thing seems impossible."

I nod. "You're right, but it'd be a mistake to give every theory the same weight. There's a big problem with unsolved cases like this one. They lead to all sorts of wild speculation and crazy conspiracy theories, especially online. There's a false equivalency that happens in the forums and posts. There's so much that's unknown and those gaps and voids and black holes get filled with outrageous and preposterous propositions based on no evidence. But because there's so little evidence, they don't get disproved either. I think if we have any chance of solving this thing and finding Aiden, we've got to focus on the evidence and what is most likely based on it."

"I'm sure you're right," Robin says. "But like I say the whole thing is impossible so . . . Anyway, y'all please keep an eye on Sheri. And try to find out what happened to him before she worries herself to death."

CHAPTER
ELEVEN

"I CAN'T TELL you how much I appreciate y'all helping with Aiden's case," Sheri is saying.

She is sitting on a wooden bench in her garden, surrounded by a thick, colorful tableau of rare flowers I can't begin to identify. Blade and I are standing before her.

There is a peaceful, calming quality to this space.

"You've built such an extraordinary space here," I say. "Such a serene environment."

"You can't imagine what I've been offered for it—well, for my home, mostly because of this, I think. It's obscene. But I could never sell. Not ever. I have to be here in case Aiden comes home. And the thing is . . . the Estates hates my garden and it violates all their rigid rules. The only reason they let me have it is because they feel sorry for me. The moment anyone else owned it, they'd make them take it down."

I look around at the delicate petals of the vulnerable plants again. They are under constant threat—from the elements, no less than the Estates.

"I still can't believe it's been two years without a single clue," she says. "How does someone vanish so completely like that—in this day and age?"

"Hopefully it's just that something has been missed, and discovering it will help unravel the whole thing."

"I have to tell y'all," she says, "I feel more hopeful now than I have in a very long time. I know y'all are . . . smart enough—no, that's not . . . y'all are insightful enough to . . ."

"Well, I don't know about that, but maybe a fresh perspective will help."

"I'm sure it will. I wonder . . . if I'll wind up not ever knowing. That's the hardest part—not knowing. I want to find him and him be alive and well, but . . . I also know the chances of that are . . . negligible at best. He wouldn't run off on his own. He wouldn't. And there's no way he wouldn't have come back when his dad died. Just no way. So . . . since there's not going to be a happy ending . . . I'll settle for having an ending. Not knowing is driving me insane. Obviously, losing him is the worst and there's no comparison, but not knowing what happened to him or where he is or who took him from me is . . . slowly driving me mad."

CHAPTER
TWELVE

PSYCHO SUZI'S occupies the front upstairs corner of a converted two-story old brick building on St. Bart's Bay in Bridgeport, a small North Florida coastal town in transition. The ancient building had housed many businesses over the years, including a fish and oyster processing plant, and the lot it sits on is still surrounded by jagged mounds of oyster shells.

"He entered here," Rick Carson is saying as he opens the door next to Red Ralph's Raw Bar, "with Brad Reed and Jade Oborne."

The three of us step inside, Blade and I both looking up at the security camera above the door as we do.

The building is empty, the businesses closed. Suzi Lankford, the owner, has given Rick a key and unrestricted access to her establishment.

Pausing a moment, we look around.

I like the idea of Ashlynn working here a lot better than Dimitri's Cloud Nine strip club.

A staircase next to the escalator, like the building itself, is rustic, weathered wood steps on an old metal frame.

A not particularly pleasant odor wafts over them and I

wonder how much of it is stale bar smell and how much of it is lingering oyster processing plant stench.

"They rode the escalator up to Suzi's," Rick says, "Aiden leading the way. He appears comfortable and relaxed and can be seen leaning against the balustrade as they reach the top."

Blade and I step onto the escalator behind Rick and the three of us ride to the top just as Aiden, Brad, and Jade had, Rick pointing out the security camera mounted on the ceiling as we are slowly conveyed to the last place Aiden Shaw was ever seen alive.

When we reach the second level, we stop and look around.

To the right is a small alcove and the entrance to Psycho Suzi's. Straight ahead is another small alcove with what looks to be a service door. To the left is a mezzanine-looking area beyond which is a walkway that leads back to a movie theater and a few shops, which at the time of Aiden's disappearance were under construction.

"As they come off the escalator," Rick adds, "they disappear from sight of the camera. They go into the bar." He leads them the twenty steps or so over to the entrance of Psycho Suzi's and through the open doors.

Psycho Suzi's smells of stale cigarette smoke, spilled beer, the sweat from a thousand patrons, and the faintest hint of pee.

Directly in front of them is a square, dark wooden bar with black barstools lining each side, an enormous stained-glass wooden light box hanging over it. The bar is centered in the large space with tall tables spreading out from it on each side. Pool tables and dart machines fill a gaming area along the back right wall, to the left a simple rustic wooden stage and a dance floor sit idle, and both the men's and women's restrooms are along the back left wall, bearing the names *Psychos* and *Psychettes* respectively.

Beer logo advertising and memorabilia fill the faux brick walls and hang from the black exposed-beam ceiling, and a huge black-and-white picture of Suzi looking her most psycho hangs high on the back wall of the stage.

"In here they drink more," Rick says. "By all accounts they had a ton to drink that night—and I can't help but think that's a factor in whatever happened to him."

"He'd certainly be more vulnerable," I say. "More suscepti-ble. Less capable. Less inhibited. He could've said or done some-thing, intervened in something, and . . ."

"We know he and Brad got into an argument," Rick says, "but we don't know what it was about. Brad won't say and those who witnessed it couldn't hear the specifics."

"He still top on my suspect list," Blade says.

"I agree he's not right and has actually been a hindrance to our investigation, but we have video footage of him leaving with Jade and never coming back. And the time between when Aiden was last seen and Brad is seen leaving is a matter of a few minutes. I just don't see how he could've done anything, and if he did, how or where he could've hidden the body without it ever being found."

"Yeah, I ain't worked it out either," Blade says, "but I ain't ready to rule his ass out yet."

"I'm not either," Rick says. "I just can't see how he could have done it. But right now I can't see how anyone could've done it."

"How early in their time here did they argue?" I ask. "I'm assuming they split up after that."

"They did," Rick says. "Brad hung with Jade—mostly at the bar. Aiden went around talking to various girls, bought shots for different groups, listened to the band, and danced. It wasn't too long after they got here."

"Everyone here that night is a suspect," Blade says, "but the bitches Aiden interacted with—and their jealous boyfriends—top the list."

"They do," Rick says, "but we haven't been able to track all of them down. Lots of people paid cash so we don't even have their names. Certain small groups and individuals were unknown to staff and other patrons."

"What about releasing images from the video and asking them to come forward?" I ask.

"I asked the sheriff about that early on in the investigation, but he may go for it now that nothing else has worked. I'll check with him again. Probably have to talk to him about putting you two on the payroll too."

Blade says, "What else went down that night? What happened next?"

"ACCORDING to both Brad and Jade, even though Aiden and Brad had words and split up, they had all planned to leave together, so near the end of the night Aiden rejoins them. The last thing he says is he's going to talk to the band and will be right back."

Aiden had loved music and playing guitar and aspired to be in a band someday.

"I can relate," Rick continues. "That's what I would've been doing. Aiden and I have that in common. I'd much rather be playing guitar in a band than investigating crime. Still don't know how I wound up doing this."

"How *did* you?" I ask.

"I was . . . My plan had been to be a teacher—always loved reading and learning—and I thought it'd be a great schedule to also be in a band. Weekends off, holidays, summer break. Done every day by two-thirty. But . . . I was robbed. Came home to find my apartment ransacked, valuable stuff missing, graffiti spray-painted on the walls. Felt like such a . . . violation. And the investigator who came out was . . . so arrogant and ignorant and . . . couldn't've cared less about what had happened to me or how I felt about it. Told me he'd write a report, but nothing would come of it and not to get my hopes up about getting my stuff back. I went in to speak to his supervisor . . . and . . . and after talking for a while . . . he offered me a job and I took it—temporarily, I thought."

"Life is like that," I say.

"I read how y'all got into this line of work," he says. "Sorry about what happened to your sister."

"Thanks," I say.

We are all quiet for an awkward moment.

Eventually Rick says, "They never saw him again. They called his phone several times, but never got an answer. They waited out front for a while but eventually left, figuring he already had. They said he'd done that before—especially here since it's so close to his mom's place where he was staying. And I should say . . . Brad and Jade's statements mostly agreed, but they were different enough not to have been coordinated. Really seems like They were telling the truth."

"What band played that night?" I ask. "What did they have to say?"

"Hobo Girl," Rick says. "Four mid-twenties guys who say they only notice the girls who come up to them. Say that's why they play—for the women. 'Cept they didn't say it so politely as me. Say a few guys always come up and want to talk music or guitars and he may have been one of them, but . . . can't be sure."

"How soon after it happened did you interview them?" I ask.

"The Tuesday after the Saturday that it happened," he says. "Why?"

"Suspicious that they are that vague about it—especially that close to it happening."

"Be worth going at them again," Rick says.

Blade says, "We know for sure Aiden went into the restroom that night?"

Rick nods.

"With as much as he was drinking . . . ." I say. "No way he didn't. Probably several times."

"Got witnesses who saw him go in at least twice when he and Brad came back later that night joined by Jade."

"Any from inside the restroom with him?" I ask.

"No, just going in."

Blade says, "How 'bout coming out?"

"Not really," Rick says.

"We take a look at the bathroom?" Blade asks.

"Absolutely," he says, and leads us through the bar, snaking through the tables to the back.

The doors to the two restrooms are next to each other beneath a huge replica of the Bates Motel sign.

Inside the men's we find a huge all-white tile room with stalls on one wall, urinals on another, and a row of sinks with mirrors above them on another. There's a retro look and feel to everything, the style of which brings to mind the most famous shower scene ever filmed. And confirming that it's no accident that it does, every wall is dotted with faux round peepholes and the eye of Norman Bates looking through them.

High on the back wall is a rectangular window—the only one on the only exterior wall in the room. It's about two feet from the top of the ten-foot-high ceiling and measures about a foot by two feet.

"That's the only window," Rick says. "Only way out of here besides the door, but . . . it's too high to reach without help or something to stand on—and there's nothing in here like that. No chairs or ladders. Besides . . . even if he could get out it, he'd have nowhere to go. There's no balcony or ledges or anything, and even though we're only on the second floor, because the ceilings are so high in here it's more like the third or fourth floor. It'd be a forty-foot drop onto the concrete. Even if it didn't kill him, he'd've had broken bones and couldn't have walked."

"No way his white ass coulda jumped into the bay from here, is there?" Blade asks.

Though the old building is on the bay, there's actually about twenty feet or so from the back wall to the water, where a concrete patio transitions to an asphalt alleyway leading to an old dock along the water where shrimp boats are sometimes moored.

Rick shakes his head. "Couldn't do it even if you have a running start and jumped with all your might."

"But what if his ass did go out the window?" Blade says. "If we considerin' everything, we got to consider that. What if he jumped and either was able to roll and not get hurt and walk away or got injured and somebody either helped him get away or killed him?"

"Except," Rick says, "the camera covering the back door and patio area would've captured him landing on the ground."

"Instead of going down could he have gone up?" I say. "Could he have accessed the roof and then come back in the building and exited some other way?"

"Theoretically . . . maybe . . ." Rick says. "But there again . . . all exits are covered by cameras . . . so even if he had . . . we'd've seen him when he exited."

"That's what it keeps coming back to," Blade says. "His body has to still be inside this building."

"Not according to our exhaustive searches and the search and rescue dogs and later the cadaver dogs."

"So he didn't leave and he's not still in here," she says.

"See what I've been living with for two years?" he says. "It's enough to drive you mad."

"We all go a little mad sometimes," I say in my best Norman Bates.

"THERE ANY BLIND spots not covered by the cameras?" I ask. "Any first-floor windows? Any service doors? Where does the band load in and out?"

"Let's start with that last one first, then we'll look at the other doors and windows," Rick says.

He leads us out of the restroom, across the dance floor, and up onto the stage.

"If Brad and Jade are telling the truth," he says, "this is the last place Aiden was known to have been going, so—"

"Needs to be looked at more closely than anything else," Blade says.

"And we have, but yeah, seems most likely that whatever happened to him happened here."

"Are there any witnesses who say they saw him over here talking to the band?" I ask.

"One woman says she thinks she saw him near the stage at some point but can't be certain."

"If he came over when they say he did," Blade says, "the band would've been breakin' down, right?"

"Right," Rick says. "They stopped playing around twenty 'til.

They have a simple set-up, use the house PA, so break down very fast."

"Is there any kind of green room backstage?" I ask.

"Two very small ones," he says.

He turns and leads us beneath the huge black-and-white picture of Psycho Suzi and through the plush black curtain into the dimly lit backstage.

About ten feet from the curtain are two small dressing rooms, no more than about ten by ten, and about five feet apart.

Blade looks down the corridor to the left. "What's down there?"

"Storage room and Suzi's office," Rick says. "To the right, down this way, is the service elevator that leads down to where the band loads in and out and where deliveries are made."

"Can we ride down and take a look?" she asks.

"Sure."

We walk down the dimly lit hallway to the old freight elevator and ride it down to the first floor.

The service elevator is open and visible. If Aiden had been in it he would've been seen.

On the first floor it opens onto a loading dock large enough to accommodate beer and booze delivery trucks and band vans and trailers. The doorway outside, which is open, is a large commercial roll-up garage door.

Rick points up to the camera on the ceiling covering the elevator. "And there's another one on the exterior of the building that covers the area in front of the door."

"Can we get copies of the video footage you have from that night?" Blade asks.

He nods. "Sure. There's a lot of it. It'll take you a while to go through, but . . . you're welcome to it. Just don't post it online or anything. Probably lose my job if you do."

"We here to help you. Keepin' everything on the DL. No one ever need to know we's involved."

"How big was the band's equipment? Did they have flight cases or any boxes big enough to hide a body?"

"Maybe," he says. "See what you think when you watch the video. But here's the thing. If they took his body out in one of their cases, they'd've had to then come back in with it a second time and get the equipment that was supposed to be in it the first time, and we don't think they did that. We searched their cases when we interviewed them. We didn't do any forensics, but there was nothing obvious—no blood or anything—and all the cases were all full of equipment."

"I realize it's farfetched," I say, "but . . . since we have no idea what happened and haven't found him or his body in all this time . . . think we have to consider everything—no matter how outlandish."

"No, I get it," Rick says, "and I'm happy for y'all to do that. I hope you come up with something we've missed. While we're here, y'all want to step out and take a look at exterior doors and windows?"

Without waiting for a response, he walks out of the loading bay, beneath the roll-up door, and out of the building.

We follow.

The moment we step outside, we encounter the briny fragrance of the bay.

"We've got this loading dock door," he says, turning and pointing to it. "It's got two cameras on the outside and one on the inside. Covers all of the loading area and most of the east side of the building."

Blade and I look up at the cameras and then back down and around.

The loading dock is in the back corner on the southeast side of the building.

Across the side street is another old two-story brick mercantile building.

Rick follows her gaze. "That building isn't open to the public. Hasn't been restored or anything. Used mostly for storage, but it has external security cameras too. Their footage will be in what I give you, as well as other businesses, but all together they only cover a small part of the area. If Aiden got out of Suzi's somehow, which we don't think he did, there's a good chance they wouldn't capture him." He turns and starts walking north up the side street. "This is the only other door on this side."

A metal emergency exit door is set back in a small alcove, a light and a camera mounted on its ceiling.

"Two significant things about this exit at the time Aiden went missing," Rick says. "This part of the building was under construction and pretty dangerous to get through—maybe even impossible given how much Aiden had to drink. And . . . the camera here at the time was motion activated. It must have a slight delay because some of the footage we have only shows the door closing—not who opened it or if they walked through it. We think it was just when someone opened it and didn't actually leave through it—if they had it would've captured them, but . . ."

Blade nods to herself as she studies the door.

"We read they poured concrete in there the week after Aiden went missing," I say. "Could his body be buried under it?"

He shakes his head. "We searched it thoroughly and had both search and cadaver dogs in there several times before we gave them clearance to continue working and pour the concrete." He looks up and points to the two windows near the top of the building on this side. "At the time Aiden disappeared, there was no second floor in this section, so there was no access to the windows on this side. And even if he could climb up to one of them somehow, why would he when he's already on the ground floor level with a door right here. Besides, no footage from any cameras—including the ones across the street—showed anyone coming out of those windows."

Blade and I look up at windows.

"We've already looked at the front," Rick says. "There's just the main entrance, which was visible by the security guards and the other patrons, so why don't we go to the back and then the other side."

We follow him back the way we came, past the loading dock to the rear of the building, beyond which is a small alleyway, a long wooden dock, and the bay, the waters of which are dark and a little choppy.

Rick points up to two windows on the second floor near the roof. "That's the window of the bathroom you asked about," he says. "See, there's nowhere to go—no ledge to stand or walk on. Nothing. If he came out of that window, his only option was dropping or falling to the concrete below, which leaves him dead or severely injured."

"Could've then been dragged over and dropped into the bay," I say.

Blade nods. "That makes the most sense—that he somehow someway wound up in the bay."

"We searched the bay pretty damn thoroughly," Rick says. "And even if we had missed him somehow, his body would've floated up and been discovered or drifted to shore. But it's all pretty moot because the cameras back here didn't pick up anyone jumping or falling from that window."

"And no evidence of any kind was found out here?" I say. "No blood? No clothing? No DNA?"

"No, nothing."

"Was a thorough search done for those things, that type of evidence?"

"We didn't run around taking DNA samples from random surfaces, but, yeah, we did a thorough search for any and all evidence—there just wasn't any. But like I keep saying, the video footage shows—"

"Video can be altered and edited," I say.

"Sure, but often not seamlessly enough so it doesn't show."

"How would you know?" Blade says.

"Okay, sure. If it's so good we can't tell, we wouldn't. But I bet it's very, very few. Let me know if you see anything suspicious and I'll see if I can have someone at the FDLE lab look at it."

The Florida Department of Law Enforcement is our version of state cops. The agency would have been the Florida Bureau of Investigation but the acronym would be FBI and that was taken. FDLE assists small departments around the state with forensics and lab work. They processed this scene and assisted with Aiden's case.

Blade says, "Doctored video footage would make this impossible crime—or whatever it is—more . . . possible."

"I'm telling you the footage hasn't been doctored," Rick says, "but y'all see what you think. Just don't share it with anyone—not even experts. Especially not experts. Let me do that part so if this thing ever goes to trial we'll be righteous. Okay . . . let's take a look at the west side of the building."

Unlike the other sides, there are no upstairs windows on this side and only one small one on the ground floor—along with one door. Both toward the front of the building.

"So not only was this door and window covered by cameras here, but they were captured by cameras on the building across the street."

Blade turns and looks at the antique nautical shop in the old metal building behind them and I follow her gaze.

"The other thing is . . ." Rick says, "this door and this window are in the restaurant and the staff was still cleaning and prepping at the time of Aiden's disappearance that night, so they would've seen him if he came through there."

"Every possibility we consider," Blade says, "has an ironclad reason why it can't have happened that way. Aiden came into the bar and never left the bar and yet isn't still inside the bar."

"It's truly an impossible crime," Rick says.

"But there's no such thing," I say. "We're missing something."

"I used to think that too," Rick says. "But after two long years of examining every aspect of this case . . . I don't know. It's enough to make me question everything—including shit as outlandish as the supernatural or alien abduction."

"You kiddin', right?" Blade says.

"Sort of."

"Just making sure."

"I'm not a kook or anything, but . . . I'm tellin' you . . . a case like this . . . it gets to you . . . Makes you question yourself, question . . . everything. And not in a good way."

I nod.

"Most investigators never catch a case like this," Rick says. "I mean . . . work long enough and you're going to have unsolveds, but not un—I don't know—possibles. I realize *unpossibles* is not a word, but I think I need new language for this case."

Having seen all the possible exits, we follow Rick back around the building, through the loading dock, up the elevator, and into the backstage hallway.

"Only things left to see in the bar are the storage room and Suzi's office," Rick says as we make our way down the dimly lit corridor.

CHAPTER
FIFTEEN

"THE STORAGE ROOM doesn't have any external exits—not even a window. Suzi's office has one window, but it's the same as the one in the restroom—no ledge or ladder or anything. Nothing to do but drop forty feet to the pavement."

He opens the storage room and steps back.

I motions for Blade to go first.

We both peer in at what looks like a liquor store—shelves and shelves of booze in a room of about 13 x 20. Beer, wine, whiskey of all types and varieties. One shelf along the back wall is filled with all sorts of beer advertisements, glasses, paper products, straws, stirrers, and coasters.

I studying the walls and ceiling and wonder again if Aiden could be inside one of the walls or up in an attic somewhere. But conclude that the stench of decay and decomposition would've been way too overwhelming to go unnoticed—even in a smelly fish house bar.

When Rick opens the door to Suzi's office, we find Suzi inside sitting at her huge black walnut desk.

"Sorry," Rick says, "didn't realize you were here."

"You're fine," she says. "Just came in a few minutes ago.

Frickin' paperwork's never done. Bane of my existence. Y'all figured out where Aiden went yet?"

"Not yet," Rick says. "Working on it."

"I don't think we'll ever know," she says. "I really don't."

"Suzi, this is Blade and Burke," Rick says. "Blade, Burke, this is Suzi Lankford."

She's a fifty-something ex-stripper with longish bleach-blond hair made unnaturally thick by extensions. Her petite, narrow frame seems inadequate to support the enormous breast implants—the majority of which are showing through the deeply plunging white V-neck blouse that contrasts her dark spray tan. Her once pretty face is a network of fine lines, but it's the hardness of her countenance and wary, dark, shark-like eyes that most detract from her potential attractiveness.

According to Ashlynn, the story on the street is that Suzi had been a stripper and then a house mom for the strippers of Jeff Holiday, a local businessman who has several illegitimate enterprises for every legitimate one, and that she only has her own bar because she blackmailed him for it.

"Blade and Burke are consulting on Aiden's case—unofficially," Rick says. "They're PIs from Panama City with a lot of experience with this sort of thing."

"God, I sure hope y'all can help figure out what happened," she says. "Can't believe how long it's been and . . . just nothing. I won't say it hasn't been good for business. We get a lot of true crime types who come in to have a drink with Aiden, but . . . I'd gladly give up the extra income to get his poor family some closure."

Ashlynn had said that Suzi had exploited her bar's connection to Aiden's disappearance in a variety of ways, including promoting it online and in social media, appearing on several true crime podcasts, and even naming a drink after Aiden—something she justifies by donating a small percentage of the proceeds to a GoFundMe campaign that supports efforts to find Aiden.

"Were you here that night?" Blade asks.

"I'm here every night," she says. "Businesses don't run themselves."

"What do you remember from that night?" Blade says.

"Did you see or talk to Aiden that night?" I ask.

She nods, her dangling earrings tinkling as she does. "Yeah, I saw him. He was a tall, muscular, good-looking guy. Stood out, you know? And I knew him from before—used to come in every time he visited his mom. Usually with a girl, but sometimes without. He talked to several that night—girls, I mean, but didn't come in with one, wasn't hanging out with just one."

"How much he drink?" Blade asks. "How drunk was he?"

"He was pretty lit," she says. "Drunk people are my business. I can tell how drunk somebody is. And he was well into tying a good one on."

I say, "So he was more vulnerable than—"

"Don't know how much more than when sober," she says. "He's a big guy and he could still walk straight, but yeah . . . he wasn't at full . . . wits or capacity or whatever."

"Did you notice if he got into any altercations with anyone?" I ask.

She shakes her head. "They say he got into it with his friend Brad, but I didn't see it. He bumped into a few people, spilled a few drinks, hit on a few girls who were here with someone, but it was all just the usual stuff. Most of the people here by that point in the night were doing the same things. I'll tell you who you need to talk to is my bouncer from back then—Serge. He was paying much closer attention to everyone than I was. I mean, if you're re-interviewing everyone. I know Rick has already spoken to all of us. Some of us several times."

Rick says, "I was thinking it'd be a good idea to let y'all talk to everyone you can without me sharing any of my thoughts or opinions or y'all reading my notes. Not color your thoughts or impressions in any way."

Blade nods approvingly.

I say, "It's possible some of the witnesses will be more forth-coming with a couple of amateurs than the police."

"I'm counting on that," Rick says. "Especially with a few of them."

CHAPTER
SIXTEEN

WHEN WE GET BACK, we find Ashlynn in tears and Sheri's small house in disarray.

"What's wrong?" he asks. "What happened?"

"I was trying to get Alana ready so I could go to a yoga class before I go to work and she wouldn't cooperate. I'm glad Sheri wasn't here to see this. She's having brunch with some of her friends."

I've seen Alana's tantrums before and the way she can turn into a tiny terror when her strong will conflicts with the one attempting to be imposed upon her.

"I . . . hate to even say it out loud, but . . . sometimes she's too much for me. I missed my class. I'm upset. The house is a mess. And she's still not dressed."

"I'm sorry."

"The ugly truth is you're better with her than I am."

"That's not true," I say, "but I'll deal with her. Is there another class you can go to?"

She nods. "Have them all the time here—like everything else. It's like ice cream cones on a cruise ship."

"Well, take your time and don't worry about anything here,

and by the time you get back we'll have the house picked up and a little attitude adjustment."

"Thank you so much. Why in the world did I ever leave PC?

"A sadistic psychopath threatened to rape and kill you and your daughter."

"Well, there's that. What am I going to do when you go back?"

"We'll figure everything out," I say. "Maybe Blade and I can retire and move here."

She laughs. "Even when we're retirement age none of us will be able to afford a place like this. Speaking of psychos . . . what did you think of Suzi?"

"The joint or the person?"

"Both."

"Very interesting. Both of them. How is she to work for?"

"Not bad. She's shady as shit but as long as you remember that . . . She's horny as hell. Always lookin' to hookup so if you get the urge to dip your wick while you're here . . ."

"I'll take a hard pass on that one."

"Was I right about the case?" she says.

"Yes, you were."

"Has similarities to that bachelorette party in PCB, doesn't it?"

"Yes, it does. I'm not sure we'll be able to get anywhere with it but we're going to try."

"That detective seems nice," she says.

"Yeah?"

"Yeah. Is he . . . unattached?"

"I'll find out."

I find Alana in her room playing with toys on her bed while watching Youtube videos about Disney princess toys on the TV on her dresser.

She protests when I find the remote and pause the video. *"Hey* . . . Turn it back on. Turn it on. Turn it on. Turn it on."

"I need to talk to you," I say.

"No, no, no. Want to watch princesses."

"Why didn't you get ready like a big girl for your mommy?" I ask.

"Don't want to."

"Sometimes we have to do things we don't want to do," I say.

She doesn't respond, just continues playing with her toys.

"Did you hear me?"

Again, she gives no response.

"Alana, I need you to stop playing with your toys and listen to me."

She gives the slightest shake of her head and continues playing.

"If you don't, you'll have to go in time-out," I say.

"No, *you* go in time-out, meanie head. You're being mean. I'm gonna tell my mommy."

"It's real important that you listen to your mommy and me," I say. "We wouldn't tell you to do something that you didn't need to do. Okay? Now, stop playing with your toys right now or I'm going to put you in time-out."

She slings the toys and flops off the bed onto the floor and begins to cry and scream while writhing around.

I move over to where she is and sit down beside her. "It's okay to be upset. Just let me know when you're better and ready to pick up your toys and talk."

She lets out a harsh little yell and kicks her feet.

"It's okay to be upset," I say again. "It's okay to yell and even kick, but it's not okay to yell or kick at me."

She yells and kicks again, but not at me.

"Take your time," I say. "Get all your upset out."

Eventually, mercifully, she stops crying, sits up, and looks at me.

"You better now?" I ask.

She nods and sniffles.

"Come here," I say, and pick her up and hug her. "Are you ready to pick up your toys in here and the living room and get dressed?"

"Will you help me?" she asks, her voice soft and raspy, coming out between sniffles.

"I will," I say. "And will you try your best to always do what mommy tells you?"

She nods.

"Cool," I say. "And when we're finished let's go see if we can find mommy a nice new boyfriend."

CHAPTER
SEVENTEEN

SERGE BIRKIN IS a legit tough guy. Not particularly big, but big enough. Not overly musclebound, but every inch of him hard as a lighter knot. He's dressed in a tight but not too tight baby-blue T-shirt and dark designer blue jeans.

He owns and operates a titty bar called Pink Cheeks in a seedy part of the south side of town. Blade and I find him bartending, bouncing, and DJing during a slow shift in the middle of the afternoon, and though the joint is mostly empty, we sit at the far end of the bar for privacy.

Earlier in the afternoon I had done a bit of matchmaking, and Rick and Ashlynn have a date planned for later tonight.

"I'll tell you this, guys," Serge says as he sets frosty glass mugs of draft beer in front of us. "I have not talked to anybody since making a statement to the police. Wouldn't be talking to you now if Suz had not requested me to."

Rumor had it that Suzi had set Serge up with this place and had a significant stake in it.

Serge looks and sounds like Eastern Bloc, his accent and speech patterns an English version of some People's Republic of Something a world away from North Florida.

"Well, we really appreciate you doing it," Blade says.

On the drive over, we had decided that we'd probably get far more and more valuable info if Blade took the lead and asked most of the questions.

"Give me moment," he says. "I will return."

He moves to the other end of the bar where three older men are seated, each with a stripper standing next to him, slowly nursing mixed drinks in lowball glasses.

Besides them, there are only three other people in the place—a stripper, the only black one here, dancing on the small, high stage in the middle of the room; a gaunt, ancient man on a high-back red leatherette lap dance sofa along the wall between the bar and the bathrooms; and the stripper sitting next to him.

Afternoons at Pink Cheeks are for older men who want extra attention and don't mind paying for it. There's no cover, half-price drinks, and the third-tier strippers who work it are not only nicer than the in-demand, pretty, young night-shift girls, but are more fully present, less distracted, and even more maternal.

"I'm gonna have to go back and forth," Serge says as he walks back up. "These guys are my most loyal and lucrative clients."

I'm surprised to hear the word *lucrative* come out of Serge's mouth, but I probably shouldn't be. His broken English is somewhat formal and he has a decent if uneven vocabulary.

"No problem," Blade says.

"Excuse me a sec," he says.

As the song comes to an end, he steps over and lifts a mic from beneath the counter and says, "Give it up for Miss Destiny."

No one gives it up or even turns to look at Miss Destiny, who is wiping down the poll and starting to dress.

"Miss Destiny," he says again. "The beautiful and exotic Miss Destiny is now available for that special trip back to the VIP room for a little extra special attention. Coming to the stage now is Miss Martha Divine."

The stripper seated next to the ancient man on the lap dance sofa slowly gets up and makes her way through the maze of small, empty tables and chairs as Serge reaches under the bar and starts the next song, which not unsurprisingly is a country song by Ashely McBryde named "Martha Divine."

As Martha Divine takes the stage, Destiny takes her place over by the ancient man on the lap dance sofa.

Serge checks on the other patrons then rejoins us.

"You want to take your stripper name from a song, fine, but one about a cheating jezebel about to be killed by the daughter of the man she's schtooping . . . These girls, man. Am I right? Anyway . . . you want to know about the boy who disappeared. What can I tell you . . . Let's see . . . He was . . . He never sat down. Not once. Like a shark . . . always swimming."

Apparently, after revealing to us what appears to be his more authentic way of communicating, he's going to stick with it.

"I'm not sayin' he didn't never stop," he continues. "He sees pretty girl, he stops, tries to chat her, you know, but he never sits, never stays in one place for very long."

"Think he was on something?" Blade asks.

"This, I do not know, but . . . my gut guess is yes . . . something. Not too . . . strong. I say . . . some form of speed, you know?"

I wonder if whatever he was on—if he was on anything at all —was from a week of staying up studying for exams or for powering through his exhaustion to party that night.

"And he was drinking too?" Blade asks.

"Like the watered-down drinks were actually water."

"How drunk was he?"

"Enough," he says. He then turns to me and says, "Hey. Man. Go tip the titty dancer on stage. Poor girl. Pair of tits like those and no one tips her. It's disgraceful. You go. Tip my girl while I talk to yours."

I glance at Blade, who gives me the slightest of nods.

"She will be fine, man," Serge says.

And even though he'll only be a few feet away, I realizes with a sinking, anxiety-inducing feeling that there isn't much I could do to stop Serge from doing whatever he wanted to—except try to reason with him or call the cops.

I stand and am about to ask Serge to break a twenty but Serge places a stack of ones on the bar.

As I reaches for the stack, Serge brings his powerful hand down on top of mine and says, "Touch her tits, ass, or snatch and I kill you . . . I'm kidding man. It's joke. Serge is being funny man. Go have fun."

I pull out my wallet and and start to hand him a twenty.

"Man, your money is no good here," he says. "Go have good fun titty time on Serge. But don't touch. Serge was not kidding about that."

I ease over to the four-foot-high stage and stand and watch as Martha Divine twirls around the pole, angling so I can still see Blade and Serge. I had been hoping to be able to hear some of what they say, but the volume of the music doesn't allow that.

"Hello, handsome," Martha Divine says, her clear, classic Cinderella slipper stripper shoes clunking loudly on the stage.

"I bet you say that to all the guys," I say. "Even old Fred Flintstone over there." I give a slight backwards nod in the general direction of the ancient man on the lap dance sofa.

She comes to the edge of the stage directly in front of me and squats down, her knees high and wide, the thinnest of G-strings covering her crotch, her bare, pear-like breasts undulating.

"Yeah, but I really mean it with you," she says with a wry smile.

I maintain eye contact with her and can see there's real wit and intelligence there.

She slides her finger down seductively and pulls open the strap of her T-back to let me place her tip beneath it.

Instead of sticking the money beneath her strap like I'm supposed to, I hand it to her, my eyes never leaving hers.

"You really not going to look at my tits?" she asks.

"It's nothing against you," I say. "*Or them*. You're lovely and they are too."

"You're not gay," she says. "I can tell that. . . . You an ass man? I can turn around."

"I'm . . . I'm not here as a . . . ah, patron."

"You a cop?"

I shake my head.

She glances over at Blade. "Oh, it's *her*, isn't it?"

"No," I say. "She's my sister, but we're working."

"Every Breath You Take" by The Police begins to play.

When I glance back at Blade again, she seems to be getting angry.

Martha Divine leans down and moves her mouth around my face and neck and to each ear, purring as she does.

"Hey," she whispers, "whatever your business is with Serge, wrap it up and get out of here as fast as you can. He's a dangerous, brutal dude. He got this place by killing a man."

"THINK SHE WAS TALKIN' 'bout Aiden?" Blade asks.

We are in the car, driving back toward the Estates.

"Don't see how killin' Aiden gets him a bar," I say. "Unless . . . Suzi had something to do with it. Maybe he blackmailed her. She blackmails Jeff Holiday to get her bar and Serge blackmails her to get his."

"Serge killin' Aiden wouldn't give him leverage over Suzi?"

"He could've done it for her," I say. "She could've done it and he helped her bury the body. I know it's farfetched, but—"

"Better than most of the other theories we've heard," she says. "Inside job would explain how he could have vanished so completely. All they'd have to do is hide the body, close up, and go home like normal. Come back the next day or whenever and . . . turn off the cameras or put his body in something that nobody would question them carrying out."

"Or hide him somewhere inside where he'd never be found —a wall or the foundation or something."

"It's the best theory so far in terms of explaining how he was never seen leaving and why he's never been found. But . . . the dogs didn't find him, so . . ."

"Wonder if he saw something he wasn't supposed to or . . . was having an affair with Suzi or if it was just an accident they covered up?"

"Doesn't explain why he or she or they would break into his mom's house in a Halloween mask pretending to be Aiden."

"True," I say, "but we have no explanation for that no matter who the killer was."

"If there *was* a killer," she says. "We don't know for sure there was. He could still be alive. That could've been *him* breaking into his mom's place."

"What else did Serge say?" I ask. "Seemed keen on splitting us up, getting you alone."

"He was mostly just hitting on me—even after I told him I was a vagetarian. And he really wants Ashlynn to come dance for him. But he did give me the names of two guys he says had words with Aiden that night, but . . . he could've just made that up to divert suspicion. He's never mentioned them before."

We reach the opulent, ostentatious entrance of the Estates and turn in.

Beneath planted palms, their fronds waving slightly in the wind, the pristine pavement shimmers in the sun as it snakes through the movie-set town with its quaint shops and manicured lawns.

"I can't get over this place," I say. "Most everything has an element of facade, but this place . . . It's all facade. It's creepy and Stepford. The way they've tried to make it look like an old town that had risen up organically and been here a while . . . Can't believe my Ashlynn and Alana live here."

I slow down as most of the vehicles around us change from cars to golf carts.

She says, "Why would a man like Serge not charge us for our drinks and actually give you stripper tipping money?"

I shrug. "Trying to distract us?" I ask.

"I think your stripper's right," she says. "I think he's far more dangerous than he seems."

"She's not *my* stripper."

"Did she give you her number?" she asks with a wry smile.

Martha Divine did in fact give me her number, but I have no intention of using it.

SHANICE WASHINGTON IS A THICKISH, middle-aged black woman, surprisingly spry and agile for both her age and BMI.

She started helping her mother clean houses when she was twelve and never stopped—not even when her mom suffered a massive heart attack.

Over the years, she has built a hugely successful business doing both residential and commercial cleaning, and has always been in high demand. These days she is the most popular over-paid maid in the Estates, but at the time of Aiden's disappearance she also had the contract for the janitorial services for Psycho Suzi's.

She cleans Robin's home every other Monday and Sheri's every other Thursday.

"Aiden was a nice boy," she says. "Always helpin' his folks when he visited. Helped me some too. All these years . . . He's about the only one who ever did. Oh, a few times here and there somebody's mama might say, 'Grab that box for Miss Shanice,' but he's the only one to ever do it on his own."

"Can you tell me anything else about him?"

"He was always sort of sad," she says. "Lost like. Didn't

mope around or make a big deal about it, but you could tell he wasn't happy. Not really. And med school and that girlfriend of his didn't help."

"Did he ever say anything?"

"No, never. I could just tell. Miss Shanice knows people. Nothin' made him light up. And this fake place don't help with shit like that. All the smoke and mirrors."

"You had the cleaning contract for Psycho Suzi's at that time Aiden went missing, didn't you?"

"For the whole building," she says. "Thought I wanted to . . . be a mogul, but . . . tryin' to get other people to work and do right . . . They ain't invented 'mount of money make that worth doing."

"Did you work anytime after Aiden disappeared?"

"The next mornin'," she says.

"See anything suspicious or—"

"A few things, but the biggest by far was the blood in the back hallway."

"Where?"

"Behind the stage," she says. "Where they bring in instruments and stuff."

"How much was there? Where was it?"

"Mostly on the floor, but a little splattered up on the bottom part of the wall. Wasn't a terrible lot but it wasn't no little 'mount neither."

"I WAS NEVER MADE aware of any blood," Rick Carson is saying. "And the crime scene team didn't process any."

After speaking with Miss Shanice, I stepped out into he front yard and called him.

"Are you sure?" I ask.

"Positive. Why didn't she report it?"

"Says she did. Told Suzi and says she's pretty sure that Jeff Holiday was there when she did. Suzi told her that she would report it to the police and for her not to clean it up."

"Did she now? 'Cause she never mentioned anything about it to us."

"Could she have said something to a deputy or a crime scene tech and you not know about it?"

"I don't think so," he says. "Because even if they had failed to tell me, it would be in their report, and in the case of forensics, and they would've processed the area. I've read every note in the file several times. I've gone over and over all the evidence collected. It just isn't in there."

"Wonder why," I ask.

"I'm gonna find out," Rick says, "but the most likely explanation is that Suzi never reported it. It's unlikely anyone in our department or in FDLE wouldn't tell me as the lead investigator, put it in their notes, or have it processed."

"If Suzi didn't report it, then the question is why," I say. "And the most obvious answer is she had something to do with it."

"Or is covering up for whoever did," he says. "And who she'd do that for has to be a very, very small list."

"She strikes me as someone who only does things out of self-interest," I say. "I think it's far more likely she's involved than she just did it to cover for someone else."

"I agree. Based on what the stripper said . . . it makes more sense that Serge is covering for Suzi than the other way around."

"And getting paid very well to do it."

"Yeah, neither of them strike me as the kind of people to do much of anything out of friendship or altruism."

"No doubt."

"This is great work," Rick says. "Y'all have already gotten info I never could. I'll follow up on this and see where it leads. What's next for y'all?"

"The band."

"Cool. Hey, are you sure about this Ashlynn thing?"

"Whatta you mean?"

"She really wants to go out with me? She's so pretty and . . . well, hot. And I'm kind of plain."

"You're sellin' yourself short," I say. "And she hasn't even seen you with a guitar in your hands yet."

CHAPTER
TWENTY-ONE

IN THE UNREAL utopia for active seniors that is The Estates, rec centers are all. The Bay Breeze Recreational Center is a huge bayside complex with indoor and outdoor components that include tennis courts, a huge swimming pool, billiards, bocce, darts, corn toss, shuffleboard, meeting rooms, picnic pavilions, dance, yoga, self-defense studios, a concert hall, and a music academy where Estates citizens can take lessons, perform, record, and pretend to be aging rock stars.

I pass by the fenced-in tennis courts where sixty- and seventy-somethings ease around the clay courts in the latest trendy tennis attire, volleying the small bright green balls back and forth. I then move through a tai chi class under one of the open air pavilions and around a belly dance class in the mirrored studio to the music academy in the back.

There I find Terrick Bushnell, the former lead guitarist and singer for Hobo Girl, finishing a guitar lesson with an eager and enthusiastic gaunt, bronzed female septuagenarian.

After telling his student how awesome she is and fawning over her all the way to the door, Terrick turns his attention to me.

"Hey man," he says. "How's it going?"

As if just having come off the stage at a huge arena, Terrick looks like a rock star, all long hair, leather, tatts, earrings, bracelets, necklaces, big black boots, and a tiny, torn vintage t-shirt that hugs his narrow man-child torso.

"Good. Good."

"What can I do for you?"

"My mom is a resident here and I'd like to get her signed up for some lessons," I say.

"Sure, man, no problem."

"I can't believe she gets to take them from you," I say. "You're the lead singer for Hobo Girl, aren't you?"

"Was, yeah. In another life. We broke up."

"Ah man, sorry to hear that. I saw you guys a few times when I was here visiting my mom. Y'all were great—especially you. What a voice."

"Thanks, man," he says. "Much appreciated."

"And the way you play," I say. "You got sweet skills, dude. You really do."

Terrick brings the long, bony, tattooed fingers of his hands together in front of his heart and bows slightly in some sort of namaste-inspired expression of appreciation.

I say, "What . . . do they have Lebron James giving basketball clinics here too?"

Terrick places his hand over his heart and bows again.

"What happened to Hobo Girl?" I ask. "Who you playing with now?"

"One of those things, man. Still not sure what happened. Was good while it lasted, but . . . All good things . . . you know? We had a . . . One of the guys, Sebastian, our bassist, crashed and burned hard . . . and sort of took us down with him, I guess. It's still a mystery to me."

"You got your own band now?" I say. "I mean, I know Hobo Girl was like *your* band talent-wise."

"I'm working on a few things," he says. "Sitting in some with other groups when needed. Doin' some session work, and . . . teaching these lessons to pay the bills while I figure it out."

"Well, let me know when you get something going. I'll be the first in line."

"Sweet. Will do, bro. For sure."

"My mom babysits for my niece a lot," I say. "What's the best age to start with for lessons?"

"Depends on the kid, man, really does. Feel free to bring her by and I can evaluate her for you."

"Oh, wow, thanks. I really appreciate that. And we're happy to pay whatever your fee is."

"Evals are on the house for Hobo Girl fans."

"Thanks, man. I really appreciate that."

"Meantime let's get your mom signed up."

"Cool. What's the most lessons a week she can take?"

"Totally up to y'all."

"Is every day too often?"

"Not at all. I like it. Jump in with both feet, you know."

The former front man for the mediocre college band charges outrageous fees for his VIP lessons.

"How soon can she start?" I ask.

"How about tomorrow?"

"Sounds good. What time do you have open?"

"Pretty much anytime she'd like."

"Cool. I'll get with her and get back with you, but I'm sure tomorrow will be great."

"Cool, man, just let me know."

"Will do." I turn to leave, but stop after a few steps and turns back around. "Hey, I have to ask . . . if you don't mind. I heard someone say you guys were playing at Psycho Suzi's the night that guy went missing. What's his name? BAiden something?"

"Aiden, yeah," he says. "No, man, I don't mind you asking."

"I just find that whole deal so . . . ."

"I know. It's like a bad joke. Man walks into a bar . . . Never walks out again. Funny you mention it . . . . That's when we started having trouble, man. Something happened to Sebastian that night. I don't know. He was never the same again."

"Sebastian? Oh, the guy you said played bass for you, right?"

"Yeah. Everyone called him Seabass. I don't know. Seemed like a pretty chill dude, but then he just changed. Never seen anything like it, and I've partied with some strange cats in my time. He just cut himself off from everyone and started trying to drink and drug himself to death. Got no idea if he's even still alive. Doubt he is, given the way he was . . ." He shakes his head and grimaces.

"Someone said Aiden was going over to talk to you guys after your last set," I say.

"Aiden—"

"Oh, right. Sorry. Aiden."

"Yeah, that's what they said and he may have, but . . . I don't really remember. You always have some guys coming up wanting to talk about your guitars or sound or what not, but . . . I started playing the guitar to get girls, you know. Didn't really notice them if they didn't have tits."

"Is it safe for my mom to take lessons from you?" I say.

Terrick laughs, then answers as if it had been a serious concern. "Perfectly safe. I like 'em young, dumb, and tight—in both senses of the word."

There are far more than two senses of the word, but I assume he means drunk and virginal, and I have a hard time keeping the disgust from my face.

"Any of the others remember Bry—Aiden? Anybody talk to him or anything?"

He shrugs. "Not really sure . . . Seems like Sammy said he talked to him, but he lies like a mother, so I don't know. This thing really didn't get big until we were already broke up."

"Anything happen out of the ordinary that night?"

He nods. "Was a weird night from start to finish. But really, what do you expect from a night like that. I really do think there's something to the veil between worlds being thinner on Halloween. It was all like black cat stuff, you know? Chaos unleashed on the world along with the tormented spirits."

TWENTY-TWO

PLAYING the part of a badass rocker chick looking for a drummer for her band and maybe a lover for her bed, Blade is sexily and stylishly clad in a black leather cropped fringe jacket, black skinny ripped jeans, a slouchy gray tee, and a pair of black leather ankle boots with four inch heels that zip up the back.

Dropping a cigarette she didn't even pretend to smoke, she mashes it out on the sidewalk with the toe of her badass boot and enters Marvin's Music Store like it's lucky to have her do so.

Marvin's Music is located in a large, old department store, its huge open space divided into sections beneath signs that identify them: Guitars—electrics hanging on most of one wall, acoustics in a temperature and humidity controlled room—Basses, Keys, Amps, Pro Audio, Drums, Accessories, Ukuleles, Sound Systems, etc.

Customers trying out new gear in each section create a cacophony of dissonant sounds that compete with instead of complement each other. Blade finds it jarring, and to her untrained ear it sounds more like showing off than test-driving new instruments.

She surreptitiously searches out Sammy Chastain, the former drummer for Hobo Girl and promptly begins to ignore him.

Wandering around in a too-cool-for-school disinterested manner, Blade acts unimpressed with everything she sees as she makes her way to the back of the giant retail space to the bulletin board hanging on the wall next to the entrance to the restrooms.

As she does, she sees a couple of young employees start to approach her, only to be waved off each time by Sammy, who makes it clear in not very subtle ways that he's interested in far more than helping her find the gear she's looking for.

When he finally makes his approach, she is tacking up a notice for a drummer on the bulletin board.

"It's your lucky day," he says.

"Oh, yeah?" she says, without looking at him, her voice thick with indifference. "How's that? Am I the hundredth customer? I win a lame T-shirt or something?"

"I'm a great drummer and I'm in between bands at the moment."

She takes a step back and examines him in his cheap black slacks and yellow Marvin's Music sports shirt complete with name tag.

"Look like a gear geek retail drone to me."

"Don't let my disguise fool you," he says. "This is totally Clark Kent shit. I'm the best drummer around."

"What, around the store?" she says, looking around the store at the mostly young white males scattered throughout.

"No," he says. "In the region. Probably farther but I'm trying to be humble and not set expectations too high."

"You're doin' just fine there, believe me."

"I really am good," he says. "Believe *me*."

She nods vigorously. "Oh, okay. Sure. I'll just take your word for it."

"I can take you over to the drum section right now and impress the hell out of you."

"Good drummers are a dime a dozen," she says. "Doesn't take a lot of skill to bang around a bit, but . . . sane, sober, serious drummers are the unicorn of the live music scene."

"You're a sexy ballbuster, aren't you? I love it. What kind of music does your band play?"

"The good kind," she says. "Any other lame-ass questions?"

"Yeah," he says. "Will you go out with me tonight?"

She shakes her head. "Not dressed like that, no."

"I won't be dressed like this," he says. "My buddy's band is playing at Psycho Suzi's and asked me to sit in on a few tunes."

"Exactly how bad do they suck?"

"Very little," he says.

"Suzi's is known for some lame-ass acts," she says.

"You can say that about every place 'cause most bands suck, but there've been some decent ones too."

"Last band that had the potential of being decent I saw there was Hobo Girl," she says, "but you could tell they were punk-ass kids and weren't about to work hard enough to live up to their potential."

"I was the drummer for Hobo Girl," he says, his voice rising an octave. "And I've been working my ass off since then. Do a lot of session and hired-gun work for major acts coming through the area."

"Oh, yeah? Would I have heard of any of these *major* acts?"

"Probably not, unless you stay current on the up-and-coming artists of tomorrow."

"What does that even mean, *up-and-coming artists of tomorrow*? That maybe one day they might be a major bullshit pop disgrace?"

"Look, you looking for a drummer or not? Have a drink with me tonight and hear me play. Whatta you got to lose?"

"Hours of my short life I'll never get back," she says. "That's what."

CHAPTER
TWENTY-THREE

I KEEP CHECKING MY PHONE.

Blade hasn't responded to my texts or calls. She was supposed to check in once she spoke to Hobo Girl's drummer.

I'm on the kitchen floor with Alana, moving between various activities, including a tea party, a Play-doh pet grooming shop, Disney Princesses coloring books, and small action figures from a Nick Jr. show about a schoolgirl vampire whose family now lives among humans and operates a Scare BnB.

It looks as if the right front quadrant of Hurricane Alana made landfall here, but the chaos is limited to the kitchen because Sheri is hosting a game night for a few friends.

"Look at this," Alana says often about whatever she's doing at the moment, especially when I glance at my phone.

At this particular moment she's coloring the dress of a long blond-haired princess I don't recognize.

"That's awesome," I say. "Blue is one of my favorite colors."

"Mine too," she says. "It's too beautiful. Hey, color with me."

"What would you like me to color?"

"Color this," she says, pointing to the long flowing locks stretched out behind the princess by the cold winter wind.

"Okay. What color?"

"Yellow, silly."

"Of course."

As we color and she hums various tunes I believe to be from the movie this character is in and makes occasional comments—some to me, some to herself—I think again about how much I've missed her.

"Would you like a dress like this?" I ask.

She stops coloring in order to consider, lifting the crayon she's holding and tapping her lips with it in a grown-up manner far beyond her years. "Nah," she says finally. "It's not my style."

Unable to stop myself, I laugh out loud.

Seeing my reaction, she repeats the line a few more times.

Many of her extraordinary and grown-up gestures, actions, and phrases are the result of her uncanny ability to remember and mimic, and I wonder where she has seen or heard something similar.

"Alana, you're so funny," I say. "Such an amazing little girl. I love you so much and am so proud of you."

Though I make a point to say these things to her every single day, she rarely responds, and on the few occasions she does, it's in her high-pitched cartoonish voice.

"*Hey* . . ." she says. "I have a great idea. Let's have a tea party."

"Let's do," I say.

As she slides over to the little tea set I bought her earlier in the day during their shopping excursion for groceries and games Sheri could play with her friends, I stand and fill the tiny tea pot with water from the tap.

When I sit down across from her and place the tea pot with the small cups and saucers between us, she lunges at me and wraps her little arms around my neck and says, "You're my best friend."

Tears fill my eyes as I hug her tightly and feel more warmth and joy than I have since she and her mother moved away.

"You're mine," I say, my voice hoarse with emotion. "I love you so much. You're such a special little girl."

"*Okay, okay,*" she says, her voice changing, taking on an *over-it* tone as she pulls away. "Let's have tea."

"You pour it for us," I say.

She does, her breathing changing as she leans over and concentrates on her task, attempting not to spill a single drop.

When she has poured both of our little cups with water from the pot, we each hold up their cups, pinkies out, and toast, each saying *bling* as their cups touch—something I had shown her once a few months ago and she has done since then no matter what we were eating or drinking. We have *blinged* plastic cups of Kool-Aid, powdered sugar donuts, Pop Tarts, juice boxes, pizza slices, and many, many other items.

Suddenly, there are four old ladies standing at the entrance of the kitchen smiling down at us.

"Oh, look, they're having a sweet little tea party," the smallest and oldest-looking of them says. I can't remember her name, but think it's something like Haddock or Hancock.

"Sit down," Alana demands. "I'll pour you some tea."

"Honey," Robin says, "if we get down there we won't be able to get back up."

"'Cause your skeletons are old?" Alana asks.

"Exactly."

In addition to her skeleton being old, Robin had spent some time on her hands and knees today, cleaning and weeding Philip Shaw's grave—something she does for her friend without her knowing it, something that would never get done if she didn't do it. Not that Sheri would ever know. She still holds such resentment against him for letting Aiden go out that night in the state he was in, she never goes to his grave.

Robin says, "Why don't you bring it in here to the dining table and let's have a tea party."

"*Yeah,*" Alana says with her typical enthusiasm. "Let's do that. Come on, Lucas."

"He'll be there in a minute," Robin says. "Miss Sheri and Miss Vivian need to talk to him first."

"You go on in there," I say. "I'll bring everything."

"Okay. I will."

I hop up and help her up, then as she bounces over to her Robin, I withdraw a cookie sheet from the cabinet, place the entire tea set on it, and follow them into the dining room area.

After I get them situated I rejoin Sheri and Vivian in the kitchen.

"Lucas Burke," Sheri says, "this is Vivian Waters. She's a dear friend of ours and has followed Aiden's case closely since he disappeared. I told her what you're doing and she wanted to tell you something."

"I told the police," Vivian says, "but I don't think they even looked into it. But of course they may have tried and been stymied by the Estates security goons."

Like Robin and Sheri, Vivian is living the good retirement life, the pale skin of her pampered face showing very little signs of her actual age. Her haircut and clothes are stylish and look like something a forty-something instead of a sixty- or seventy-something would wear. And like so many of the residents, she is observant and knows far more about what's going on around here than the Estates security give them credit for.

"My boy, Jackson, is handsome like you," she says. "He's also sweet and good with children. Such a good boy. He's also a gay."

Sheri says, "Gay, not *a* gay."

"Huh? Oh. Well, anyway. Not sure if that's relevant but I think it might be. Anyway . . . He was here visiting me and also went to that Suzi bar for the Halloween party the night Sheri's Aiden went missing. Such an odd phrase, *went missing*, isn't it? Anyway, he didn't think too much of it at the time, but he did later—after everything. He said an older man in a gay pirate costume with a big fake beard that covered most of his face was staring at him most of the night. Say he thinks he remembers him staring at Aiden and a few others too. He used the word *lasciviously*. He bought a lot of drinks for people that night—all men. My Jackson was one of them and he thinks Aiden was too, but says he can't be sure. Anyway . . . My Jackson was drugged that night. He can't be sure it was by the gay pirate guy but he believes it was. If one of his girlfriends—he has several of those, girls who call him their gay BFF—hadn't seen how out of it he was and got him home safely, I don't know what might have happened."

"Maybe the same thing that happened to my Aiden," Sheri says.

"When he got back to mine," Vivian continues, "he was so out of it. You could've done anything to him. We had to half carry him in. I called security and reported it, and they said Suzi's was out of their jurisdiction but they'd look into it and notify the sheriff's office. When we didn't hear back from them, I called the sheriff's office myself a few days later. They said they had never received a report, but that they would look into it and talk to Estates security and get a copy of my original report. Never heard back from any of them and got nowhere anytime I called either of them again."

"We just thought you should know," Sheri says. "In case it's relevant to what happened to my Aiden."

"We will definitely look into it," I say. "That's very good to know. We'll also try to find out why nothing was done by the authorities."

"Who's *we*?" Vivian asks. "Do you have help?"

"I have a partner named Blade and we're actually working with the lead investigator of the original case, Rick Carson."

Sheri says, "Ashlynn is on a date with him right now."

"He seems like a nice young man," Vivian says. "That's great. And maybe you'll be the help he needs to finally solve the case."

CHAPTER
TWENTY-FOUR

"THIS THE PLACE where that guy went missing," Blade says, looking around.

She and Sammy are seated at a high-top table not far from the dance floor, waiting for the band to start.

"We were playin' that night too," he says.

"Bullshit."

"We were," he says. "Was a weird night all the way around. Halloween party. A cluster from the jump."

"Which one of y'all killed him?"

"Not me. That's all I can say for sure."

"Too bad," she says. "You could definitely be my drummer then. Nothin' more rock 'n' roll than murder."

He studies her for a long moment, seemingly trying to determine if she's serious. "Do I have to have killed a man or—"

"It's not a requirement or anything, but it'd guarantee your spot."

"What about helpin' a friend hide a body?" he says. "What's that get me?"

"Little more cred for sure," she says, "but . . ."

"What?"

"Anybody can say anything," she says. "Doesn't mean shit."

A young, skinny cocktail waitress with big fake boobs and no ass wearing black athletic shorts and a white Psycho Suzi's wife beater approaches them, order pad up, pen at the ready. "What can I getcha?"

The only thing more unflattering than the way the odd-shaped shorts fit her narrow frame are the supposed skin-color tights beneath them.

Sammy turns to Blade. "Buy me drunk and I'll tell all—including where the bodies are buried."

She looks at the waitress. "I'll have a dark and stormy."

"Moscow mule for me," Sammy says. "Thanks."

Looking at Sammy for the first time, the waitress's eyes widen. "Hey, Sam the Man. You playin' tonight?"

"Just sittin' in on a song or two."

"Cool."

She hustles off.

"So you didn't kill the Shaw guy, but you helped dispose of his body?" Blade says.

"That is not what I said."

"You did a good job," she says. "Two years and not even a whiff of him. You drum as good as you hide bodies, you hired."

"I hide bodies as good as that . . ." he says, "I'm not about to tell you or anyone else where they are or that I had anything to do with it."

"So it's all just bullshit."

"Guess you'll have to figure that one out for yourself."

"Unless I get you drunk and loosen up those girly lips of yours."

"Girly?"

"Don't tell me no one's ever told you you have puffy, bee-stung, girly lips before?"

"People tell me they're big and sexy, but not girly."

"Might want to start hangin' with more honest peeps," she says. "Or not . . . If your feelings are as girly as your lips."

"What is wrong with me?" he says. "You're beating the absolute shit out of my balls and I'm lovin' every minute of it."

She nods. "Also fits with the girliness. Some loser beats the shit out of them and all they can do is clean up the mess and beg for more."

"Daaa-mn," he says. "I'd hate to meet the bastard who turned you into . . . this."

"Wasn't just one, I assure you."

She hops down off the tall chair, forgetting she has four inch heels on, and nearly goes down.

"You *leavin'*?" he says, the pitch of his voice rising and filling with disappointment and desperation.

"Simmer down, sweetheart," she says. "I just have to pee."

She makes her way over to the restroom without busting her ass, takes a moment to gather herself, splashes some water on her face, careful not to mess up her rock 'n' roll makeup, then returns to their table.

Though only gone for a few moments, by the time she gets back their drinks have arrived and the band is playing.

He raises the little copper cup his Moscow mule is in and says, "To badass rock 'n' roll bitches."

She points for him to put his drink down and he does. She then pushes hers over to him and takes his. "In case you slipped some date-rape shit in mine."

"If I did, that mean you're gonna date rape me now?"

Before she can respond or make an alternate toast, the song ends and he is called to the stage.

She sits down and begins to drink his drink as she listens to him play. She wouldn't know good drumming if it bit her in the tit, but the song sounds good and his playing neither stands out nor detracts from it, which she supposes is good.

He plays three songs, during which time she finishes off his drink, and by the time he reaches the table she feels so sleepy and out of it that she finds it hard to hold her head up.

CHAPTER
TWENTY-FIVE

I TEXT BLADE AGAIN.

I'm starting to get worried. She should've checked in by now —actually, way before now. The music store has been closed for hours.

I wonder if Sammy Chastain is the killer and if he has Blade.

She's more than capable of taking care of herself, but if he surprised her, got the jump on her before she knew what was happening . . .

When she doesn't respond to my text, I try calling again. When I get her voicemail, I leave another message. "Please call or text to let me know you're okay. I'm getting worried."

I think about calling Rick Carson, but don't want to interrupt his date. Besides, I'm being an alarmist, overreacting at this early stage.

It then occurs to me to check Sammy Chastain's social media.

Bingo.

His most recent Facebook post says he's sitting in with a band at Psycho Suzi's tonight.

TWENTY-SIX

AS I AM PULLING into the parking lot of Psycho Suzi's, I see Sammy and Blade about to pull out.

At least I think it's Blade. It's hard to tell. Not only is she dressed like a rock star, but she's draped over Sammy like a— actually, she looks passed out.

As soon as I'm in the parking lot, I find a place to turn around, and when Sammy pulls his flashy red Kia Soul into traffic, I am right behind him.

As I follow Sammy far too closely, I reach into my pocket, pull out my phone, and call Rick Carson. After several rings it goes to voicemail.

"I hate to interrupt your date and I could be overreacting, but Sammy Chastain just left Psycho Suzi's. Blade is in the car with him and she looks unconscious. I'm following him now. We're headed east on 98. Call me back as soon as you can."

I wonder if I should call the sheriff's office and report it, but decide to give Rick a few minutes to return my call first.

Traffic on the coastal highway is relatively slow and sparse. I'm following far too close not to be seen, but I'd rather Chastain spot me than take a chance on losing him. It's not like this is some sort of surveillance operation. I'm trying to keep Blade alive. Rick can deal with arresting and making a case against Chastain.

Chastain turns off 98 onto a desolate rural highway.

I follow.

The dark two-lane rural route is straight and flat and lined with acres and acres of planted slash pines—very few of which were damaged or destroyed by Hurricane Michael, the Cat 5 superstorm that decimated the region a few years back. Somehow this swath of timber had escaped largely unscathed.

I phone Rick again and leave another message updating him on where we are now.

As I'm ending the call, I nearly slam into Chastain, who is turning onto a dirt road that runs diagonally back toward the southeast.

I keep going straight on the highway after Chastain pulls onto the dirt road, but only for a short distance. As soon as Chastain's red running lights disappear into the woods, I stop, make sure nothing is coming in either direction, then turn around and head back toward the road.

Tapping 911 into my phone, I press the speaker button and drop the phone onto the seat.

As I turn onto the dirt road, I try to make out the numbers on the lopsided mailbox.

Just as the 911 operator comes on the line, Rick begins beeping in.

"911. Where is your emergency?"

"I had called Investigator Rick Carson first and when I couldn't get him I called you, but he's calling me back right now. I'm going to click over and take his call. And then he or I will call you back."

Without waiting for a response, I click over.

"I got your message," Rick says. "Where are you now?"

"A dirt driveway off 386. He just turned onto it and I'm following him."

"Okay. I'm on my way and I'll get deputies rolling. Wait for us if you can—unless her life is in imminent danger. We should be there in ten minutes or less."

When I reach the end of the driveway, I see Chastain's car parked in front of a small rustic cabin, the driver's side door open.

Wishing I had a weapon or anything that might be used as one, I pull behind Chastain's car and gets out, leaving my car running with the lights on.

Approaching the other vehicle, which is also running with its lights on, I see that the driver's seat is empty. Walking a little farther, I see that Blade is still inside, slumped over, seeming unconscious.

"Blade," I say. "Blade."

She doesn't respond.

I run around to the passenger side and try to open the door only to find it locked.

Rushing back to the driver's side, I press the unlock button on the open door.

Running back around to the passenger side, I stumble and trip over something on the ground and fall face first.

As I turn to get up, I see it was Sammy Chastain who has tripped me and is now holding a handgun on me.

"Stay down," Sammy says.

His voice is high and tight with tension, his eyes are wide and crazed, and the revolver is shaking in his hand.

"Why are you following me?" Sammy says. "What do you want? Did you drug her?"

"She's a friend of mine. I was worried about her. Why is she passed out? What are you doing with her?"

"I don't know, man. I'm just . . . She's . . . tripping on something. I don't know what she took or if someone slipped her something. I don't know. But . . . wasn't me. I . . . I'm just trying to help her."

"By bringing her here?"

"I didn't know what else to do, man. I don't know her. She

has no ID on her. Nothing."

"Why didn't you take her to the hospital?"

"I don't know. I just panicked. I didn't want them to think I had anything to do with this. I'm on probation."

"Can I get up?" I ask.

Chastain takes a few steps back. "Yeah, sure, but don't try anything. I'll shoot you if you try anything, and you're trespassing on my private property, so . . . you know . . . Stand Your Ground and all that."

"If you're telling the truth," I say, "I'm sure you won't mind if I check on her."

"That's fine. Just go slow. I'll be right behind you with the gun pointed at your head."

I lift my hands as I turn around and slowly begin to make my way back around to Blade.

I've only taken a few steps when I hear sirens.

"You called the cops?" Sammy asks.

"Yeah. Again, it shouldn't be a problem if you're innocent and telling the truth."

"Yeah, cause no innocent people ever got jammed up by the cops."

"Not many white ones," I say.

When the lights start flashing in the trees around us, Sammy takes off running into the woods.

I rush over to the front passenger door, snatch it open, and pull Blade up.

"Hey, are you okay?"

Her eyes roll back in her head and she mumbles something incoherently.

I gently slap her face and shake her a bit, raising my voice as I say her name again and ask her to wake up and stay with me.

A few moments later, I'm surrounded by deputies with their guns drawn, yelling at me to slowly raise my hands and back away from the vehicle.

"HE SWEARS he didn't drug her and was just trying to help her," Rick says.

"Why'd he run?" I ask.

We are standing out in the hallway in front of the open door of Blade's hospital room. It is later that night. I have been here with Blade the entire time. Rick and Ashlynn have just arrived.

"You said he had a gun, right?"

"Yeah."

"Well, he didn't when we found him. Probably ran to get rid of it."

The small community hospital is quiet, its hard-surfaced hallways dim and empty.

I look at the two of them standing there all dolled up. "How was the date going?" I ask.

"I thought it was just about perfect," Rick says, then looks at Ashlynn.

"It was the best first date I ever had until you called and ruined it," she says.

Rick beams and nods. "Me too. Not even close."

"Sorry about that," I say. "If I had known it was going that good I wouldn't have called. I'm sure Blade would've been happy to die so y'all could finish it."

"You think he was going to kill her?" Rick asks.

"I don't know," I say. "You really want to help someone, you ask for help there at the bar. You call an ambulance or you take her to the hospital. You don't take her to your secluded cabin."

"Yeah, it's sketchy. And yet . . . I'm inclined to believe him."

"Really?"

"He's begging us to give him a polygraph," Rick says. "And with his phone call, he didn't call an attorney. He called Suzi and asked her to show us the video footage from tonight that proves he didn't put anything into her drink. And I'm gonna tell you . . . it looks like he spent most of the time they were there playing drums with the band. Wasn't even with Blade much."

Ashlynn says, "Maybe he's actually telling the truth."

"Might just be," Rick says, "but either way . . . there's not a lot I can do. Unless we find video footage of him doing it or a witness comes forward . . ."

"Could you search his house and car for whatever drug she was given?" I ask.

"Not with what I have now. It's not like on TV. I can't get a warrant with what we have."

Blade sits up in the bed, and we rush in to her.

"The hell am I? What happened?"

"You're in the hospital," I say. "You're fine. Someone slipped you something at Suzi's."

"Ain't that about a bitch," she says. "Help me get up out of here."

Rick shakes his head. "You need to rest and—"

"I'll rest at Sheri's," she says. "Ain't stayin' here."

"I'm afraid you can't," Rick says. "You've been—"

"Uh, I'm afraid I can and I'm going to if I have to fall out of the bed and crawl my black ass down the hallway."

"We'll help you," I say. "Here, let me help you up."

I step over and extend my arm to her.

"She really needs to stay for observation and—"

"But she's not going to, so . . ."

"Okay," Rick says. "But at least let a nurse come and discharge you."

"They take way too long. I'm leaving now. Sorry to be such a bitch about it, but I've got to go. I need my clothes," she says.

I step over to the wardrobe and grab her clothes.

"And I wasn't drugged," she says.

"It affects your memory, but you were," Rick says. "Sammy Chastain says he didn't do it, but—"

"He didn't," she says. "I wasn't drugged. And he didn't drug me. Because *he* was the one who was drugged."

TWENTY-EIGHT

"I DIDN'T DRINK MY DRINK," Blade says. "I drank his. He drank mine and was fine."

"So somebody at Suzi's is drugging guys," I say. "Could be what happened to Aiden."

"I'm gonna go look at the surveillance footage," Rick says. "Especially around the bar. 'Cause it sounds like whatever was put in his drink happened before it ever reached the table. Hopefully Suzi will let me poke around behind the bar too."

"I can help with that," Ashlynn says. "I work tomorrow."

"Thanks," Rick says to her. I appreciate that, but . . . I don't want you getting involved. It's too dangerous."

"It's too dangerous for me, but not for y'all?"

"I just meant somebody at Suzi's is up something bad. Whoever it is . . . I don't want them to even know you know."

"But having an inside woman has got to be a big advantage."

"It is, but it's too dangerous," he says.

"Think of Alana," I say.

"You're more of a mom to her than I am, and I don't see you being careful."

"Well, I am. I'm too careful sometimes."

"His ass sure is," Blade says. "That shit's dangerous too—like driving too far under the speed limit."

"I just don't want anything to happen to you," Rick says. "I'm really looking forward to a second date."

"Well, there won't be one if you don't let me help," she says. "I'm the one who started all this. I want to help find Aiden for Sheri."

"Okay, okay. Just be careful and make sure nobody knows what you're doing. I'm gonna head over to Suzi's now to look at the surveillance footage."

"And I'm comin' with you."

"Only question is . . ." I say, "is it continuation of your date from earlier tonight or a second one."

Ashlynn says, "Depends on how it goes. I'll let you know."

"I'll be in touch," Rick says. "You get her home safely and take good care of her. We'll regroup soon."

With that the two of them walk out of the room.

"I'm gonna need some help gettin' dressed," Blade says.

"No problem. Just tell me what to do."

"I'm just weak and sort of out of it."

"I won't look. Just tell me how I can help."

"My ass ain't really concerned about modesty at the moment," she says. "Or ever. Besides you my motherfuckin' brother and I just want to get out of here."

After I get her dressed, I say, "Anything else? Purse? Wallet?"

"Nothing identifying," she says.

"That's what Sammy said—why he wasn't able to take you home."

"Didn't want to run the risk of having my cover blown," she says.

"What's your sense of Sammy?" I ask.

"Think he tellin' the truth about everything, but that don't mean he wasn't involved in what happened to Aiden."

TWENTY-NINE

"WAS IT HIM?" Sheri asks.

Her voice is quiet and flat like she doesn't expect it to be.

Blade and I have just entered her dark, quiet house to find her sitting at the dining table waiting for us.

Or maybe she's waiting for Aiden.

I shrug. "Don't know for sure, but don't think so."

Blade says, "It look like he not even the one who drugged me tonight."

"Really?"

I can feel my weariness at a molecular level. I'm completely depleted, and all I want to do is crawl into bed, but I'm sure Blade feels even worse.

I turn to Blade. "Why don't you go get in bed and I'll catch Sheri up on what we know?"

"Never intended to do anything else," she says. "Night."

"Need anything?" I ask.

"Maybe some water when you get a minute. No rush. It's for later."

"You got it."

She disappears into the darkness, and I step over and take a seat across the table from Sheri.

"The guy tonight, Sammy," I say, "seems more likely the intended victim than the perpetrator."

"*Really*?" she says. "How in the world?"

I tell her.

"Oh wow," she says.

"With what Vivian said about Jackson earlier tonight," I say, "it makes me wonder if someone is drugging men at Suzi's and if it could be connected to what happened to Aiden."

"He was such a big, strong boy," she says. "I've always wondered how someone could've overpowered him. I've always thought maybe if he were drunk and there was more than one attacker, but . . . if . . . It would make far more sense if he were incapacitated."

When I stumble into my room, I find Alana fast asleep in my bed, which brings a smile to my face.

I ease into bed beside her, attempting not to wake her, but when she opens her sleepy eyes slightly, says my name, and hugs me, I'm glad I did.

I feel guilty for spending less time with her than I had planned to today. She needs so much right now.

I've never had my own child, but that's what she feels like to me. I don't just adore her, I feel responsible for her.

Aiden's case is consuming too much of my time and attention right now. I'm not spending enough time helping parent Alana, and I've got . . .

I'll do better tomorrow, I tell myself as I fade into the underworld of the unconscious.

CHAPTER
THIRTY

ACE DAVIS IS a former Florida State football player who, thirty years after his collegiate career ended, still has big, broad shoulders, a trim waist, and a general muscular thickness everywhere, particularly in his arms, neck, chest, and hands.

He's wearing clothes tailored to accentuate his impressive build, including a green blazer with the Estates logo embroidered on the left breast pocket.

He walks with intention, as if he is always needed for something important, and perpetually has a radio in his huge right hand.

As the head of Estates security he wields a lot of power, but no matter how much it is, he carries himself like it's far more, like maybe he's top cop of the free world.

"Mr. Burke," he says, tossing his radio to his left hand and extending his right.

I shake his huge hand and appreciates that he doesn't try to establish his dominance by crushing my smaller one.

We meet in front of the Estates security headquarters located in the back of a building of quaint retail shops, which like everything else in the Estates looks both new and pristine and yet like it has been here for decades. A pipe and tobacco shop, a confectionery, an upscale toy store, a high-end toggery, and a golf shop all front the huge building with no other markings on it.

If Davis hadn't told me about it when he told me where to meet, I wouldn't have known it was here.

"I appreciate you meeting with me," I say.

Blade is still asleep, still recovering from last night, still waiting for the drug to wear off.

"My pleasure," he says. "My job is not just to ensure our community is the safest in the world, but to reassure our residents and their families that it is by showing them how we do it."

I had asked to meet with the Estates head of security under the guise of questioning Sheri's safety.

"If you'd like to come with me," Davis says, "I'll show you just how safe Miss Sheri really is."

He leads me over to a John Deere Gator utility vehicle that has been repainted and branded with the Estates logos and badges.

"Hop in."

Davis drives like he walks, as if the fate of the world rests on him getting where he's going as fast as he can.

I buckle in and hold onto the *Oh Shit* handle mounted on the side as Davis races through the Harbor View town square with its huge faux lighthouse in the center, beneath the movie marquee touting both classics and the latest releases, and around the many restaurants and shops, most of which are Estates-customized versions of national chains.

Unbidden but not unwelcome, thoughts of Lexi and Heather drift through my mind, and I feel a twinge of something akin to homesickness.

"Notice the street lamps," Davis says. "See how they're shaped."

I examine them. "Yeah."

"Each and every one isn't just a light, but a camera. The same is true of traffic signals, signs, shop facades, certain trees—especially around the golf courses. Most of those we added because of what happened to Aiden, even though it didn't happen here."

Leaving the square, he races toward the recreational center.

Slowing down a little in front of the huge sports and recreational complex, he says, "Look at that. See all the safe, active seniors?"

I look at the wealthy, white, vibrant retirees playing tennis, pickle ball, shuffleboard, and corn toss, practicing tai chi, and taking dance, yoga, and exercise classes—all before the backdrop of the beautiful bay and beneath the benevolent sun shining down on them from a cloudless sky.

"Yeah," I say.

"Not only are most of the instructors trained in security, but there are always Estates security personnel mixed in the crowd. We look like civilians, an adult son or daughter here visiting, but we're armed, highly trained security specialists. When we say this is the safest place on the planet, we mean it."

I nod and give the middle-aged muscle man an *I'm impressed* expression, but I'm actually troubled by the corporate big brother presence and surveillance state tactics on display unbeknownst to the tennis, shuffleboard, and pickle ball players.

Davis speeds off again, this time taking us to the front gate. Each Estate community has its own name, theme, architecture, and its own main entrance with a gatehouse and a guard.

"The real threat—not that there are any *real* threats to our security system—are from without," Davis says. "That's why we closely control who comes in. That means vetting the residents— though that's mostly done by the price tag."

I feel nauseous at the monied exclusivity implied in that statement.

"But it also means checking and double-checking everyone who comes in," he continues. "We don't have riffraff here—not as residents or guests."

I laugh to myself, thinking that's exactly what Blade and I are —riffraff invaders.

"You mentioned that the enormous costs of living here prevents socioeconomic diversity, but I've noticed there's not a lot of racial diversity or—"

"We don't exclude anyone on the basis of race, religion, political affiliation, or sexual orientation," Davis says, "so if there's a . . . Well, let me put it this way—our communities are self-selecting. Some have more diversity than others, but we certainly don't do anything to create a quota, incentivize, or artificially inflate some sort of ridiculous ideal of diversity concocted by some ivory tower professor somewhere way up north."

I try not to react to his bullshit rationalization for the wealthy white utopia they have constructed here along the Redneck Riviera where so many live well below the poverty line.

"We can lock this place down in seconds," he says. "No one in or out—and all from the command center."

I nod and act impressed. "Could I see that?" I ask. "You've shown me the cameras. Can I see the feeds?"

"I'm afraid civilians aren't allowed in there—for security reasons. You understand. Hell, most of my staff never get to go in there. Where are you parked? I'll drive you back to your car."

He whips the Gator around and heads back in the direction of the security building.

"What about Sheri Shaw's son, Aiden?" I says. "How did a member of this community vanish off the face of the earth like that?"

"Technically, he wasn't a member of this community," he says. "Just visiting. But even given that . . . it would've never happened if he had just remained within the safe confines of the Estates. I can't police and protect the whole world—would that I could—but I certainly can and do for everyone inside this citadel."

"But surely someone in your position with your experience and expertise has a theory about what happened to him."

He shakes his head. "I don't trade in theories and speculation, only facts, and unfortunately we don't know all the facts in that case. And probably never will. It's a sad business, but it's outside of my circle of responsibility, which is this amazing community right here. Just look at it. It's so beautiful and vibrant and safe."

"But what about the attack on Sheri?" I say. "That happened here. That has us worried about her safety."

"Our investigation is ongoing so I can't say much about it, but I will tell you this—you have nothing to worry about. Sheri is safe. It was an isolated incident and it's specific to Sheri and what happened to her son. It has become a very public case and there's a world full of crazies outside of the gates of this great place. But rest assured . . . the perp will be brought to justice. I'm seeing to that personally."

THIRTY-ONE

"WONDER if they can see us right now?" Rick asks.

"Probably," I say, and turn and wave toward the trees lining the golf course.

We are standing behind Sheri's house.

"It's so surreal that they have it," Rick says, "but then to boast about it like it's something to be proud of . . ."

"It was sickening."

"So much concentrated power," Rick says. "You know they never have turned over the costume Sheri's attacker wore. I'm telling you . . . they do what they want to . . . with impunity. Those who live here have far more to worry about from them than the supposed boogie men outside these walls they're meant to be protecting them from."

"No doubt," I say, "and—"

I stop as Blade opens the recently repaired back door. "You boys gonna hang out in the garden all day or y'all wanna do some investigative work?"

We walk over and join her inside the house.

Sheri, Ashlynn, and Alana are at a yoga class, a spa day, and a playdate respectively, so we have the house to ourselves.

Blade sits down at her open laptop on the dining room table.

We join her.

"How're you feeling?" I ask.

"Like the fuckin' fog is finally liftin'," she says, "How'd it go with Ace Davis?"

"Feel free to ask him yourself," I say. "He's listening in right now."

"Huh?"

I explain.

She shakes her head. "Not surprised. But he's wrong. Our presence here shows the riffraff can still get in."

"Says if Aiden had just stayed inside the confines of this citadel he wouldn't've gone missing," I say.

"How that jibe with what happened to Sheri inside her own bedroom inside her own house inside his citadel?"

"Riffraff from outside must have snuck in somehow, but not to worry, top cop is on it."

"Always an outsider, ain't it?" she says.

"Stranger danger," I say.

"Bet he black too," she says.

"The danger is always out there, always from the other."

"Statistically, you're far, far more likely to be hurt or killed by someone you know," Rick says. "It's not even close. And yet . . . what happened to you last night . . . seems like the work of a stranger. We can find no evidence that Sammy did anything. Of course, I haven't found any evidence that anybody else did either."

"If Sammy's been going to Suzi's for years," I say, "why just drug him now?"

"Good point," Rick says.

"Maybe Sammy *wasn't* the intended target after all," I say. "Or maybe he's been drugged before."

"That's interesting," Rick says. "Both of those could be the case—or maybe Sammy was meant to be drugged so he'd be incapacitated when whoever did it made his move on Blade."

"I been thinkin' some of those same things," Blade says.

"I'm still going over all the surveillance footage to see—"

"You mind if I take a look at it?" she asks. "See if I recognize anyone?"

"Not at all," he says. "That's a great idea. I'll get the files to you."

She says, "I've been watching the feeds from the night Aiden vanished. Look at this."

She angles the laptop so we can see it too.

"Still have a lot of footage to look at," she says, "but I wanted to go ahead and show y'all this . . ."

She clicks on a short clip of one of the external doors in which nothing happens. It's less than ten seconds and could be a still photograph, for all that takes place in it.

"What am I missing?" Rick says.

"Nothing," she says. "Nothing happens in it. Absolutely nothing. But . . . something had to trigger it. Some movement made the camera come on and start recording. I read something that said these cameras were notoriously slow to start capturing footage. What if the something that triggered it was Aiden leaving through this door, but he did so so quickly that he was gone and the door was already shut again before any footage was captured?"

"Interesting," Rick says.

"Could'a been a feather or a piece of trash blowing by, but . . . What if instead of just Aiden leaving . . . it was Serge Birkin leading or taking Aiden out? He might know that if he did it quick enough it would go unrecorded."

I nod. "Could be."

"Thing is . . ." she says, "it's the only shot like that from that night. But I went back to look at other days of this same door— we have footage from the day before and two days after—and two different times it's the same exact footage except . . . in one of them you can just make out the door closing, which would seem to confirm that someone could've exited and the camera wasn't triggered quickly enough to capture it."

I say, "The camera is outside and is set to come on when the sensor detects motion. If someone were entering the building, it would be triggered by them walking up, putting the key in the lock, etc., but with someone exiting . . . it's going to be triggered when the door opens, but it only takes a fraction of a second to pass through a door, so it could completely miss the person leaving."

"Two more things," she says.

She minimizes the file of the door and brings up footage from the loading dock and elevator feed.

"Check this," she says, starting to play clips of the band loading out.

Hobo Girl can be seen carrying instruments and pushing large flight cases—two of which are large enough to hold a body.

"We had said if they put his body in one of these cases . . . They'd have to take it back in to get the piece of equipment that was supposed to be in it . . . but . . . look at this. They roll both these cases out, load all their equipment, and then a good bit of time passes—over an hour. It's very late. The bar has been closed for nearly two hours. The band is not drinking or anything. They've been loaded for a while, but they don't leave. Why? Then two strange things happen. First, this case is pushed out and loaded. Why so long after the others? But that's not even the most interesting part. I went back and watched the footage from them loading in. They only have two of these large rolling cases, and they've already loaded them like an hour before and then somehow they roll another one out. But it's not just another. I think it's the same case. Look."

She brings up two videos side by side. One shows the two cases being rolled out when all the other equipment was being loaded. The other shows the single case being rolled out by itself an hour later.

"See the one on the left," she says. "Look at the stickers. Look at the scuffs and paint and the way the band name is stenciled on it. I think it's the same case."

"Looks like it is," I say. "Your brain ain't foggy at all."

"And check this shit out . . ." she says.

She pulls up another clip.

"While that case is being pushed out and loaded into the van in the back by the guitarist and singer Terrence Bushnell, Thompson Tait, the rhythm guitarist, is carrying this piece of equipment—which has no case or covering of any kind, and it certainly looks like it needs one—out the front door. But because he's exiting with the bartender and staff, it's easy to miss him and the fact that he's with the band. When they loaded in, he came in with everyone else. Why didn't he leave the same way? Why would he walk out the front door carrying a piece of equipment, and where did he go?"

CHAPTER
THIRTY-TWO

THE COPACABANA CLUB is a '70s-themed bar and dance hall inside the Estates.

Lit with black lights and lava lamps and decorated with psychedelic-patterned posters, disco balls, macrame owls, and Farrah Fawcett pin-up posters, the smallish club is filled with a purple haze of incense and tobacco and pot smoke.

Each dark retro round table surrounding the dance floor has an earth-tone fondu pot and a CB radio at its center, and four green, brown, and gold retro leather chairs around it. The CBs are how the patrons place their orders.

Beyond the tables, in the shadows along the back walls, a series of waterbeds serve as groovy seating.

The house band at the Copacabana Club, The Frayed Bell Bottoms, look like they're at a hippie-themed Halloween party or maybe a casting call for a live-action remake of Scooby-Doo. There are bell bottoms, of course, but also mini skirts, maxi dresses, tie-dyed everything, and plenty of headbands, scarves, chokers, and wood, stone, and beaded jewelry. All the guys in the band have huge hair, big bushy mustaches, and sideburns, and the female lead singer is sporting a Dorothy Hamill wedge.

When Blade, Sheri, Robin, and I walk in, the band is playing Marvin Gaye's "What's Going On."

Thompson Tait, the former rhythm guitarist for Hobo Girl, is now the bassist for The Frayed Bell Bottoms. Blade and I are here to try to talk to him. Robin and Sheri are here because when they heard Blade and I were going asked if they could tag along.

As soon as "What's Going On" ends, the band goes right into Blondie's "Heart of Glass."

Seniors with various degrees of stiffness and immobility awkwardly move around the dance floor—at least half of them in some form of '70s attire.

As soon as we get Robin and Sheri situated at a table with drinks, Blade and I hit the dance floor.

Dressed in '70s attire, our plan is to make a splash with our enthusiasm for all things '70s, then approach the band on their break.

We dance to the end of Fleetwood Mac's "Go Your Own Way," then all of Michael Jackson's "Don't Stop 'Til You Get Enough."

I lean in and say, "It's like we're at our parents' class reunion."

"Yeah," she says. "If we had parents."

The band plays a slow song I'm not familiar with next, and Blade and I dance awkwardly like brother and sister, leaving plenty of room for the Holy Ghost between us.

"Hope we're doin' as well as most of them when we're their age," I say.

"We aren't even doin' that well now," she says, "and no way we make it to their age."

As sad and sobering as it is, I know what she's saying is true.

"Talkin' to the members of Hobo Girl who are easy to find is fine," Blade says, "and maybe they were all involved in some way, but you know as well as I do that the one who's exhibited the most post-crime change in behavior is the most likely to be our guy."

I nod. "Sebastian Lewinsky," I say.

From what Terrick said in his statement and from what we've read and seen online, Sebastian Lewinsky acts like someone who killed someone that night.

"Lookin' at the situation and how they all acted following that night, I'd say if they had anything to do with it at all, Sebastian did it and the others helped him cover it up."

I nod "We've got to find him. But we also need to know what his former bandmates have to say about him."

As the song ends and we stop dancing to clap for the band, the lead singer, a young woman named Kat, announces that they'll be taking a short break, but not to go anywhere because they'll be back soon with more groovy tunes.

Before the band can get off the stage, Blade and I are there.

Handing her business card to Kat, Blade says, "I'm Blade Beattie and this is Lucas Jennings. We own a string of clubs throughout the southeast and would like to talk to you about playing at them. I have no idea what a small place like this pays, but I'd be shocked if we couldn't quadruple it. Are y'all full-time? Do you play anywhere else? Do anything besides the '70s stuff?"

"We're not full-time," Kat says.

"But we want to be," Thompson adds.

"We can make that happen," I say. "We've launched more than a few careers. We have enough clubs so you can play at a different place every night for three weeks—and they're close enough that you won't be in your van all day getting to the next one."

"We also do an '80s and '90s set," Kat says. "That's just because we play at two other theme clubs inside here."

"Y'all are good," Blade says. "Nice and tight. With a really smooth vibe. You really should be playing for a hip audience that's not half dead. And y'all should know . . . our Nashville area clubs regularly have record producers in attendance. Do y'all have an agent or manager? Do you do any originals? Is a record deal something you'd be interested in?"

Thompson says, "Hell, yeah. I've got lots of original songs."

"You look familiar," Blade says. "I can't quite . . . put my finger on it, but . . . I feel like I've seen you somewhere."

"You've got her card," I say. "Let us know if you'd like to come in for an audition. I'm tellin' you . . . you get the gig and it'll change your lives."

"This is probably a long shot," Blade says, "but might as well mention it. We're in the process of producing a true crime TV series for Oxygen about crimes committed in or around bars and clubs. The budget is unbelievable. There's no money like TV money. So if y'all ever played in a place while a crime was being committed . . ."

As soon as the band had stopped playing, John Lennon's "Imagine" had come up on the house system, and now Pink Floyd's "Comfortably Numb" is playing.

"I have the greatest true crime club case of all time," Thompson says.

"Oh, yeah?" Blade says, sounding dubious, skeptical, unim-pressed.

"Yeah. Aiden Shaw."

Blade says, "That's where I know you from. You played with Hobo Girl. Good band, man. Didn't recognize you with all the extra hair and the porn 'stache."

He nods and rubs his head.

"Y'all played the night Aiden vanished, right? That's one of the stories we're covering in our series. Suzi's given us full access. We planned to get one of the members of Hobo Girl to be in it. You got any juicy info . . . inside information or anything? If you do . . . Oxygen pays fifty-grand for a single interview—a buck fifty if we come back to you."

The rest of the band fades away, drifting off to take their break, as Thompson Tait edges to the front of the stage to stand directly in front of us.

I say, "If he has anything at all I bet we can get him three. Didn't Shaw say—wasn't one of the last things he said was he was going to talk to the band?"

"That's right," she says. "Wonder if they'd want the full band?"

"Why, when we could save a cool mil by just interviewing the one who'll talk the most?"

"No, that's true. But they'd probably prefer to have the one who dropped off the grid . . . what's his name? Seabass."

"He won't talk to you," Thompson says. "But I will. And I can tell you everything he could."

Stevie Wonder's "Superstition" comes on, and the elderly men in leisure suits and the women in their disco outfits take to the floor.

"Whatcha got for us?" Blade says. "We get a finder's fee for you, but we won't go back to Oxygen without knowing what we have."

"How about this?" he says. "Sebastian Lewinsky killed the poor bastard and Terrick Bushnell and Sammy Chastain unknowingly helped him cover it up."

CHAPTER
THIRTY-THREE

"THOMPSON, THIS IS—" Blade says, attempting to introduce Rick to him.

"I know who he is," he says, his dismissive tone thick with derision.

Rick's presence may derail the entire thing, and I wish we hadn't called him to join us.

It's much later, and Blade, Thompson, Rick, and I are standing behind the Copacabana. Robin and Sheri had wanted to wait for us, but we convinced them they needed to go home and relieve Alana's babysitter.

The dark night is turning cool following an early evening rain. A brisk, biting breeze blows through the trees lining the golf course across the way.

"He's a consultant on the show," Blade says. "Worked the original case. Has the best working knowledge of it. He was able to retire recently because of what we're paying him."

"Oh," Thompson says, his voice and attitude changing.

"We use him as a kind of human lie detector," she says. "But he also follows up on any info that comes in. Attempts to verify it before it goes into the show."

"So tell the truth," I say.

"I will, man. Swear. Got no reason to lie. But . . . do we need to sign a contract or something?"

Blade pulls out her phone and tells Thompson to do the same.

"Record this with your phone too," she says, raising hers up in what looks like the selfie angle. "You recording? Step in here with me. This is a legally binding contract between Glamour Girl Productions and— What's your name again?"

"Thompson Tait."

"If Mr. Tait has truthful and useful information we can confirm, he's entitled to an on-camera spokesperson's commission of no less than thirty thousand. Do you agree?"

Thompson nods. "I agree."

"Do you agree to tell the truth, the whole truth, and nothing but?" she asks.

"Yes, ma'am. I do."

Blade is so convincing I almost begin to believe what she's saying.

"Tell us what you got," she says.

"I ain't just gonna tell you everything for free," he says.

"Not asking you to," she says. "Just tell us enough to convince us you're worth paying a hundred Gs or more and putting in our show."

"Well, let me start by sayin' I didn't have anything to do with it," he says. "Didn't even know anything about it at the time. I ain't an accessory or whatever you call it—not even after the fact. I don't know for certain, so I'm not . . . I can't be arrested or jammed up in any way over any of this. These are things I put together later—after the events of that night, after learning that Aiden Shaw went missing. Okay?"

Blade nods. "Absolutely."

He looks at Rick.

Rick nods. "You can't be held responsible for something you weren't involved in. From what I understand you sayin' . . . all you have is a theory anyway."

"Yeah," Blade says, in her bored and disappointed voice, "not sure that's worth paying for."

"Now wait just a minute," he says. "I have firsthand inside information."

She says, "Okay, well, let's hear it."

"It was such a weird night," he says. "Strange and eerie from jump street. It was Halloween and the weather was all funky—most bizarre rain I've ever seen—but it was more than that. Nothing went right. Everything was off. I realize that can't be one person's fault, but . . . it all began and ended with Seabass. Sebastian Lewinsky, our bassist. I don't know if he was on something or just having some sort of breakdown, but he'd never acted like that before. Always been a pretty quiet and chill dude. Not that night. That night he was demon possessed or something. And think about this . . . we had been in a band together for four years, known each other for five or six, were friends—not close, but friends—had spent time together a minimum of three days a week for four years . . . and after that night none of us have ever seen him again. Aiden Shaw wasn't the only one who vanished that night."

"Not once?" Blade asks.

He shakes his head. "Not a single time. Tell me he didn't have something to do with it. And how about all that stuff about that night? Halloween and the rain . . . it's gonna make good TV, right? And I can describe it better, more . . . you know . . . fancy or picture it or poetry like or whatever. I can see it. Can't you see it?"

"We're gonna have to have more than pretty words and pictures," Blade says. "You got anything else or not?"

"Yeah. 'Course. I's just settin' the table. Now y'all come on in an' eat."

"Look," Blade says. "We got somewhere to be . . . so . . . get to it or let us go."

"Okay, okay," he says, "but just know I got all kinds of cool details and sub stories or whatever. There's a lot I can share.

Anyway, the things is . . . that guy, Aiden, he came up to us when we finished playin'. Always have some that do. It's mostly women, thank Christ. Most nights we only went home alone 'cause we wanted to. But there'd be an occasional guy—usually wanted to talk about being in a band or guitars or tell us about some songs he had written. I remember this guy because he wanted to talk about all that stuff and he also wanted to help us tear down and load out, but he was pretty damn drunk. He was sort of a big guy—tall anyway, and could've been a help. We almost always used some of these talkie-talkie dudes as roadies, but he was so wasted—and that's sayin' something 'cause we all had been drinking a lot too."

"Was he too wasted to help?" I ask.

"Let's put it this way . . . I didn't want him anywhere near my gear, but . . . he was one of those who insisted, you know? Wouldn't take *no* for an answer."

"Why didn't any of y'all tell me any of this back when it happened?" Rick asks.

He shrugs. "No offense, man, but it ain't our job to do your job. Plus, well . . . the others were more directly involved. I figured one of them would tell you. And, hey, you weren't offering three hundred grand. No, seriously, I just . . . I don't know man. But I'm tryin' to do the right thing now. We both are, right? And we're both getting paid for it, so . . . win-win, right?"

"Keep going," Blade says. "He was wasted and wouldn't take *no* for an answer."

"That's right," he says. "I put my guitar in my case and got it out of there fast. He kept trying to help. I said, 'I got it. See if anybody else needs help.' He kept on. He knocked a few things over. Thankfully only like empty stands and shit, but still . . . And he just wouldn't go away. We were tryin' to talk to some girls, but he kept gettin' in the way and we had to keep grabbing our stuff before he could. Everybody was pissed at him and askin' him to leave but he wouldn't. Seabass said something to him—like piss off or something—and Aiden grabbed the girl

Seabass was trying to talk to and kissed her long and deep, puttin' his hands all over as he did. And she started doin' the same thing to him. When Seabass tried to pull him off her, Aiden slung him back and he fell into his brand new bass and knocked it off its stand and it snapped the neck. It was brand new—a several thousands of dollars instrument—and it was ruined. Seabass threw it in its case and stormed backstage with it. Aiden followed like apologizing and shit and that's the last we ever saw of him. Disappeared behind the curtain and never came back out."

"That doesn't mean Sebastian Lewinsky killed him," Blade says.

"No, it doesn't, and I ain't accusing anybody of anything, but . . . if he didn't . . . why'd he do such weird shit with the equipment and—"

"What do you mean?" Blade asks.

"He comes back in a while later—without Aiden—and he grabs one of the large flight cases and rolls it back behind the stage. He's never so much as touched one of those before and now he's gonna load it—but he doesn't. Didn't know that until later, but he didn't load it. Later, when we have everything packed up—and he never came back in to help during that time —we start rolling our shit backstage and find him there. Not only has he not loaded the case, he's removed the equipment that was in it. He says he's takin' that equipment home to work on 'cause it's got a hum or a buzz or something—something none of the rest of us heard. Then get this— He says he's put some of his personal shit in the case and so put his own padlock on and please don't mess with it, he'll swap it out later. You may or may not think this sounds odd, but if you knew him you'd say this was the most bizarre thing he's ever done. All of it. Just nuts. He never worked on equipment. He never took any initiative. He never did shit. Then . . . if all that ain't nuts enough . . . he says he's going out the front. Now, he did have his own car that night, but . . . he parked in the back by the van. So what in the hell would make him go out the front just to have to walk all the way around? All this . . . taken with how he was never the same again and he's gone off the grid . . . I'd say he did it, but even if you don't think he killed him and put his body in the flight case—"

"What happened to the flight case ?" Rick asks.

"He came and got it later that night," he says. "Just took it off the van. Didn't ask. Didn't tell anyone. Didn't— The van was parked at Sammy Chastain's place. He's got a secluded cabin in the—"

"Oh, we know," Blade says.

"I think all of this is things your audience will be riveted by, but . . . just for the sake of argument let's say there's a reasonable explanation for everything he did . . . he'd still be the last person to have seen Aiden alive."

"TELL me we're not saying Aiden was killed over breaking a bass guitar," Blade says.

"People've been killed for less," I say. "But I don't think that's what we're saying."

We are driving back home from a long night at the Copacabana Club, looking as if we're driving back from 1977.

Before leaving, we had determined that Blade would examine the video footage again to see if any of it corroborates what Thompson Tait had said, Rick would try to track down Sebastian Lewinsky, and I would reinterview Terrick and Sammy to see if we can confirm any of Thompson's claims.

Blade says, "Probably will come down to some trivial shit like that, but . . ."

"Could just be what started everything and something else happened in the back," I say. "Or maybe it didn't have anything to do with it. Won't know until we track him down and we may not even then."

"True."

"He could've witnessed something," I say. "He could be hiding out of fear."

"Aiden or Sebastian?"

"Either. Both. But I was talkin' about Sebastian."

"Could be dead," she says.

"He certainly could," I say. "Whatever the case . . . finding out should help us get that much closer to finding out what happened to Aiden."

"I know it's possible, but it's hard to see how the two disappearances aren't connected."

When we arrive in Sheri's neighborhood, I pull over in front of her place and park in the culdesac out front since there is no room in her small driveway.

As we climb out of the car, Serge Birkin steps out of the darkness and stands in front of us.

I take a quick look around. Serge is alone, and though he no doubt has a weapon on him—likely more than one—none are visible. And yet his presence and his seemingly innocuous words carry a palpable menace, an undeniable threat.

I wonder if the Estates security surveillance monitoring team is watching us right now. Even if they are, can they tell Serge is threatening them or does it just look like three people having a normal conversation?

"Look at you two," he says. "Hippie dress, no? And Halloween is not yet I think. This how do you say . . . dry run? Pre-game?"

"What can we do for you, Serge?" I ask.

"I was just wondering . . . how much pain you two have experienced. I do not mean what passes for pain in the first world. I mean true, existential pain, the kind that makes a man happily betray all that he considers holy. I know, I know, it is hard to imagine such pain in a place like this, but I assure you, it is possible everywhere, even a place like this."

Blade's hand had already been in her '70s-era macrame handbag searching for the key to Sheri's house when Serge had stepped out of the darkness in front of them, but it wouldn't matter. She's got knives and blades hidden all over her body.

"Say as just . . . ah, a hypothetical . . . How much pain do you think you could endure before begging me to hurt her instead? It is interesting question, is it not? Here is another . . . Do you think you could stop me from hurting her?"

"I could," I say, "but I wouldn't have to."

"Oh, yeah?" Serge says.

"The question is would I stop her from hurting you and the answer is no."

He laughs but looks at Blade again.

"Hippie dress for Halloween and you attempting to do tough-guy things. You see the problem, my man? You are not tough guy and yet you are attempting to do tough-guy activities. It is very confusing. So it is simple—"

With one quick motion, Blade steps forward and slices Serge's left leg open.

"You don't have long to get a tourniquet on that and get it stitched up before you bleed out," Blade says. "If you take the time to do anything else—even talk more bullshit to us, you're dead."

Without another word he unbuckles and pulls off his belt, forms a tourniquet on this leg and limps off into the dark night.

"Good to know we're getting somewhere," I say. "He wouldn't have felt the need to threaten us if we weren't."

"Exactly," she says. "But who was he threatening us for—just himself? Suzi? Sebastian and the band? He didn't come threaten us after we spoke to him or Suzi—only after we spoke to Thompson and the other band members."

"One of them could've tipped off Sebastian and he sent Serge. No way to know. But I don't like him knowing where we're staying and what that means for Alana, Ashlynn, and Sheri's safety."

"He's probably been keepin' an eye on Sheri already. Could'a been his ass that broke in the other night."

"I think she would've mentioned his accent."

She shrugs. "Yeah, if she could make it out with him whispering."

"But even if it wasn't him," I say, "he could be behind all of it —or at least the one doing the dirty work for whoever's really behind it. But I still don't understand the purpose of the break-in. Can't see how it fits with . . . 'Course I can't see how anything fits right now."

"OH MY GOD," Sheri says. "Well, y'all have to stop immediately. No way I'm taking a chance on losing someone else. Can't risk anything happening to little Alana."

She and Robin had been waiting up for us, anxious to find out what we learned from Thompson Tait—an interest that had faded when we told them what had just happened.

Before we had come inside, I had called Rick to let him know what happened and to warn him about possible attacks from Serge. Rick was infuriated and promised to take Serge down—and until he did, to provide some protection for Sheri, Ashlynn, and Alana.

"What kind of people are these?" Sheri says. "So dangerous. I just can't believe my Aiden would be mixed up with people like this."

"Wouldn't have to have been for them to have been involved in what happened to him," I say. "Could've been wrong place wrong time. Stumbled onto something. Saw or heard something he wasn't supposed to. I'm sure you would've mentioned it, but . . . the masked guy who broke into your house and claimed to be Aiden . . . he didn't have an accent, did he?"

She looks up and closes her eyes as if attempting to access

her memory. Twisting her lips and frowning in concentration, she eventually shrugs. "I'm not sure. I . . . I guess it's possible. He was whispering and I was so scared that all I could hear clearly was my heart thumping in my ears. But . . . there could've been a slight one . . . that may be why I knew it wasn't my Aiden. I'm just not sure."

I nod. "It's okay. I just wondered if it might be Serge, but . . . it's hard to see why he would."

Robin says, "Makes no sense. But y'all don't have to worry about that anymore. Just let the police figure it out and deal with it."

When Sheri opens her eyes, she looks at Robin.

"You okay?" Robin asks her.

She shrugs again. "Okay enough."

"We can keep y'all safe and keep working the case," Blade says. "'Specially with Rick's help."

"And he's agreed to give ya'll protection," I say.

"We'll do things more low-key and in the background from now on," I say. "As far as Serge will know we quit."

"If he's even still with us," Blade says.

I nod to her and look back at Sheri. "I really want to talk to Brad, Jade, and Amanda. They've been refusing to talk to anyone —reporters or police—but . . . maybe if you asked them . . . as a personal favor to you . . . if they'd speak to us off the record . . ."

"I can ask," Sheri says. "I think Amanda would. Maybe Jade, but I doubt Brad would, but . . . all I can do is ask."

"I don't think you should," Robin says. "I think y'all need to let the police handle it."

"Police haven't been *handling* it at all," Blade says. "No offense to Rick, but we've already gotten farther than anyone has. We need to keep going."

"It's too dangerous," Robin says. "And not just for y'all, but for all of us."

Sheri says, "Is there anything I can do to help? I know I'm an old women, but . . . I'm not completely useless."

"I really appreciate it, but . . . I can't think of anything. I don't want anything to happen to you."

"I don't either, but . . . I've lived a long time. Most of my life is behind me. And since I lost Aiden . . . hasn't been much of a life. If something happened to me . . . wouldn't be nearly as tragic as if something happened to you young people."

"That's so brave and kind of you, but just staying safe and keeping an eye on Alana and Ashlynn will help so much. And reaching out to Amanda and Jade and Brad."

"What is it?" Ashlynn says. "What's goin' on?"

We turn to see her standing behind us.

I tell her.

"*Fuck*," she says. "This is why I left. Why I can't be in your lives. It's too dangerous for Alana. If it's not Dimitri it's someone else."

"You asked us to look into this case," Blade says.

"That was a mistake," she says. "I don't know what I was thinking."

"Someone was most likely murdered," Blade says. "You didn't think there would be bad people involved? You didn't think they'd not take kindly to us looking into what happened?"

"Why can't y'all just—"

"We'll protect y'all," Blade says. "Nothin's gonna happen to you or Alana."

"I can't deal with this right now. I'm going back to bed and probably have nightmares."

"Everything's gonna be okay," I say. "We won't let anything happen to y'all. I swear."

"So y'all will protect us," she says. "Just like y'all did Brooklyn Hill?"

I open my mouth but nothing comes out.

"We won't be the only ones protecting y'all," Blade says. "Look at it as gettin' to spend more time with Romeo Rick."

Without another word, she turns and re-enters her room.

"She'll be okay," Sheri says. "Things will look better in the morning."

I feel guilty for exposing Ashlynn and Alana to more danger, and part of me wants to take them far away from here.

"I know it's late and we need to go back to bed," Sheri says, "but I have to ask. Did y'all get more good information tonight?"

"Think so," I say and give them the highlights. "Seems like Sebastian Lewinsky, Hobo Girl's bass player, is the most likely to have been involved. He was the last one to be seen with Aiden and since that night he has exhibited the most suspicious post-offense behaviors."

"The what?"

"The way someone acts following a crime," I say. "The post-offense conduct. The way someone acts can actually suggest guilt. It's often used in court—especially in sentencing—but I'm using it purely psychologically. Observing how people behave following a crime can give us insight into their state of mind. Most people who commit a crime act differently after it. The more significant the crime, the more significant the change in behavior. That's for people with a conscience. For sociopaths, psychopaths, and other such organized nonsocial offenders, the crime can actually become a type of game. These offenders often return to the scene of the crime for the gratification they get out of it, and reach out to either taunt or offer to assist the authorities in the investigation. From a psychological standpoint and post-offense conduct alone, I'd say Sebastian needs to be our prime suspect."

Sheri shakes her head and blinks back tears. "I want him to be alive somewhere, but if that's not possible . . . I don't want him to have lost his life over a damn guitar or a stupid barroom brawl. I still just feel like this is all my fault. I should've never left that night or should've come back when Phil told me how strange Aiden was acting before going out."

"You can't blame yourself," Robin says.

"Well, I do," she says.

"I'm more to blame than you," Robin adds. "I'm the reason you weren't here."

I say, "It's highly likely that being here wouldn't've changed anything."

"I've never said this to anyone and I really don't want the authorities to know," Sheri says, "but I think Aiden overdid it studying for his exams and all the pressure he put on himself for medical school. I just didn't realize it at the time, but looking back . . . Given the way he was acting, I think maybe he was taking something to keep him from sleeping and to help him focus—and whatever it was, coupled with not enough sleep and all the intense stress he was under and then all the drinking that night . . . had him behaving so bizarrely. I don't want anyone to know. I don't want that to be his legacy, but it may have contributed to what happened to him. And as much as I blame myself for what happened . . . I blame Phil even more. I've always felt like he should've stopped him from going out that night, that he should've called me sooner and let me know how exactly Aiden was acting, but he didn't. It was only later that night right before bed when he called to say good night, and even then what he said was vague and didn't come close to telling the real story of how strung out Aiden really was. If he had called me sooner . . . If he had been more accurate in his description, more honest about his concerns . . . I would've jumped in the car and driven back right then."

"He knew that," Robin says. "It's why he wasn't."

"That's why I didn't have a funeral for him—Phil, I mean. Why his grave marker is so small and generic. Plenty of blame and guilt to go around. God, I just want to wake up from this nightmare . . but I never will and I know that now. And I'm resigned to that fact."

"EVER BEEN in a relationship where you loved the person more than they loved you?" Amanda asks.

I nod, though I don't think I ever have.

"It's . . . it can be painful, but mostly it's just there in the background—something you only think about occasionally when something is said or done or not said and not done to remind you."

Amanda Woods, Aiden's college girlfriend, is a small, sweet, petite kindergarten teacher who dresses nice and smells good. She's got straight blond hair, big blue eyes, pale white skin, and bright red lips. She looks like a modern, cool kindergarten teacher—not the schoolmarms I had when I was a kid.

She had agreed to speak with me as a favor to Sheri, but insisted I come to her classroom and said she could only give me a few minutes.

Though there's an underlying and essential sadness to Miss Amanda, I doubt that any of her little students ever see it. I'm willing to bet that with them she's as effervescent as the bright, bold colors of the letters and images on her many bulletin boards.

While I'm interviewing Amanda, Blade is guarding the others.

"Aiden and I had a trip planned for that Monday," she says. "Did you know that?"

I nod again.

"Even though he had disappeared and wasn't responding to calls or texts, I still showed up at the airport, bags packed, ready to go on our adventure, hoping against every voice inside my head that said he wouldn't be there, that he wasn't just missing but was already dead. I waited and waited—long after we missed our flight, long after Philip and Sheri tried to get me to leave. God, they were so . . . broken. Just . . . devastated. They knew as well as I did he hadn't just gone off somewhere and lost track of time or was sleeping like a dead man because he hadn't slept the week before. We knew. And still I sat there in that little airport until it closed. Didn't know what else to do."

"I'm so sorry."

She dabs at the corners of her eyes with a small pink tissue, sniffles, and clears her throat.

"Sorry to bring up such painful memories," I say.

"It's always with me," she says. "Always. I'm sure you've heard all the people in the true crime community speculating he was going to propose to me on our trip to Miami. Well, he wasn't. He had no interest in getting married. I'm not saying I was a placeholder girl exactly, but . . . he was never going to marry me and we both knew it. It's amazing all the things people theorize without any evidence or proof at all."

"Yes, it is."

"Some of them also say I had something to do with it," she says. "They see that footage of him talking to those girls outside a few minutes before the bar closed and . . . think I killed him in a fit of jealous rage or something. Doesn't matter that I wasn't here. I knew Aiden slept around some. Did I want him to? No. Of course not. But I knew that was part of the . . . price, I guess, that I paid to be with him. He didn't do it a lot. But he was always looking. He was always horny as hell and he was a big, good-looking guy. He never had to look far. Between us . . . I'd be surprised if what happened to him didn't involve a girl. But I never got jealous. He never denied me . . . anything. Never neglected me. And when I was around he was with me—not anyone else, not even looking. It was just when we were apart that he . . ."

I nod and wonder if that's really the case or a whitewashed version of it.

"Do you know that I kept calling and texting his phone?" she asks. "Every day. Without fail. Left messages until I filled his inbox and couldn't leave any more. Called and called and called."

Aiden had still been on his parents' plan and Sheri kept paying the bill hoping he might answer someday or that the authorities might be able to check his phone.

"In all that time he only picked up once," she says. "Well, not him, but whoever has his phone. It was on his birthday, which . . . I don't know . . . makes me think whoever killed him knows when his birthday is, but . . . why answer it and not say anything? Could've just been a coincidence, but it's hard to believe it was. "

He thinks about what that might mean. Is it possible Aiden's still alive? Did he start to answer her in a moment of weakness because it was his birthday? Or is his killer a sadist—enjoying torturing Amanda, waiting each day for the phone to ring, the messages to come through? Of course, it could be possible that Aiden is alive but being held captive and his captor wanted to inflict even more pain on his birthday.

"People say I moved on too quickly since I'm with someone else now, but I didn't move on for a very long time. At least it felt long to me. And what I did, I did for survival. And between you and me, if by some long shot hail Mary against-all-odds miracle he showed up alive . . . and would have me back, I'd go back to him in a heartbeat. And I think my Steve knows that. But see, he loves me like I love Aiden. I'm not going to be in a relationship where I'm the one who loves the most again. I can't. It's nice to be on the other side. It's not exactly what I thought it would be, but . . . this is about survival."

"Can you tell me what he said or texted you that night?" I ask. "Was any of it suspicious? When you look back on it now, does anything seem to have a different meaning?"

"It was pretty much the usual stuff," she says. "Any time he was out drinking and I wasn't with him he'd get super horny and sweet. He'd call just to say he wished I was there, or that he wanted me, or would I please jump in the car and come join him. Stuff like that. The longer the night went on . . . the more explicitly sexual he'd get."

"Did you ever go and meet him?"

She nods. "A few times. Depending on how far away I was and how early in the evening he started asking me to. I'm . . . a bit of a people pleaser in general, but when it came to him . . . I had a hard time saying no to anything he wanted."

I start to say something but she continues.

"He said if he ever even thought about going out with Brad again to slap the shit out of him and remind him of what a douche he is. He said Jade was okay, but he hated the way Brad treated her. I suspect . . . he either had a thing for Jade or they had slept together at some point in the past. I don't know that, but I think most of his and Brad's arguments were over girls— even when they both had girlfriends."

"How intoxicated would you say he was?"

"Extremely," she says. "Even for him. I'd say he was on something besides booze too. He didn't really do drugs—except when he was prepping for projects or studying for exams. I don't think he had slept more than a few hours in a week. And the later it got, the worse he got. Slurring his words. Being loud and belligerent. Not making sense. One of the last things he said to me was something about being a better guitarist than the guy in the band and maybe takin' his job. Showin' Brad . . . something, maybe that he wasn't a joke or something like that. Didn't even say he loved me when he hung up—and he always did that. The very last time I heard his voice, his last words to me ever and they were a garbled, muddled mess."

THIRTY-SEVEN

"DOESN'T MATTER WHO ASKS," Jade Oborne is saying, "Brad won't talk to you. Nothin' personal. He won't talk to anyone. He's even stopped talkin' to me."

Jade Oborne, Brad Reed's former sometime hookup, is the only female beautician at an old-fashioned barber shop in Bridgeport.

"Why do you think that is?" I ask. "What's he hiding?"

"Why's he have to be hidin' something? What if he told all he knows when it happened and doesn't know anything else? Should he just keep sayin' the same thing over and over or start making shit up?"

"Those are the only options. Most people know more than they think they do and being asked different questions by different people can sometimes help bring it out."

"Or make them make shit up," she says. "It's been two years. You forget things. I can't be sure of what's true anymore. You read stuff. You hear stuff. It all runs together. You forget what's what. If I's you . . . I wouldn't believe anything I've got to say."

"Would you be willing to undergo hypnotherapy?" I ask.

"What? Why? No."

"Everything you saw and heard that night is in your mind," I say. "Hypnosis is a way of accessing it. It can unlock what's hidden away."

"*No way*. Don't want nobody muckin' around in my mind."

"It'd be a trained professional who knows what she's doing," I say. "Not a cop or a—"

"No way. No how. Nobody—don't care who it is. Ah man, just thinking about that has me freakin' out. Now I'm stressed as hell. I can't talk about any of this anymore right now. Can we talk more later? Sorry, man but . . . I just can't right now."

CHAPTER
THIRTY-EIGHT

ALANA IS AGITATED.

She has picked up on her mother's anger and anxiety and is acting out.

I'm trying to think of ways to help her, to calm her down, refocus her, change her energy.

"I have a great idea," I say, using the same words and inflection she does when she wants me to do something with her.

She doesn't respond.

"Let's play trick-or-treat."

She looks up at me for the first time, interested, intrigued.

"It'll be good practice for Halloween. You get your jack-o-lantern bucket and I'll get behind a door with some candy."

She bounces up. "Yeah, let's do that."

I quickly grab her bucket and some random items out of the cabinet, and we rush over to the guest room Blade and I'm sharing—though last night I slept on the floor in front of Ashlynn and Alana's room.

"Okay, knock on the door and say trick-or-treat."

I enter the room and close the door.

A moment later I hear a soft little knock that melts my heart.

I slowly open the door and say, "Happy Halloween."

Her head is back and she is looking up at me with the sweetest, happiest little expression, her mood completely transformed.

"Who do we have here?" I ask.

"It's a little princess," she says, the slightest hint of a lisp making her words all the cuter.

She has no costume, but what she has that continues to amaze me is an impressively well-developed imagination.

"What a cute little princess."

Extending her bucket forward, she says, "Happy Halloween. Trick-or-treat. Can I have some candies?"

"You certainly can, Little Princess. Here you go."

I drop a Tootsie Pop, a peppermint, and a package of microwavable popcorn into her little pumpkin bucket.

"Happy Halloween, Little Princess," I say. "Hope you get a lot of candy."

"Happy Halloween," she says. "Now, let's do it again."

"Okay," I say, "I'll close the—"

"Luc . . . I . . . I've got to pee."

"Okay," I say. "Let's go. I'll race you. On your mark . . ."

She drops her bucket and gets into her little runner's stance.

"Get set," I continue. "Go."

As usual, she wins the race, and like always I ask, "How did you get so fast?" as I help her pull down her pants and panties and set her on the seat.

She normally says either "I just did" or "At the fast store," but this time she says, "I have fast powers."

"Yes, you do," I say. "The fastest fast powers on the planet."

"We live on planet Earth," she says.

"Yes, we do."

"Mars is a planet," she says. "It's hooo-ooot."

"Yes, it is."

"I have pee powers too," she says.

"Yes, you do," I say, letting out my delight in amused laughter. "Yes, you do."

AS BLADE and I sit across from each other at the dining room table, scanning surveillance footage on laptops, she looks up and says, "We should stage a reenactment of the night Aiden vanished at Psycho Suzi's with as many of the original players as we can get."

"Yeah," I say. "I like it. I meant to tell you . . . When I was speaking to Amanda and Jade I had the thought we should see if we can get Suzi to have a Hobo Girl reunion show on Halloween, try to get everybody who was there that night back."

"Hell, yeah," she says. "I like the idea of doing it on Halloween. Maybe we can combine that with the reenactment. Think anybody'll go for it?"

"I have some ideas on how we might get them to," I say. "Let me call Rick and see what he says."

I grab my phone and call Rick as Blade returns her attention to the surveillance footage.

Without preamble, I pitch him the idea.

"I like it," he says. "I do, but it's dangerous . . . Too much liability. Too many things to go wrong. I couldn't . . . I don't know what I'd do if something happened to . . . well, anyone, but especially you or Blade since I recruited y'all."

"We're not talkin' about anything official or that you'd be on the hook for," I say.

"That'd be even more dangerous than if we ran it as an official operation with plenty of help. I'd rather do it that way. Maybe I could call in some favors and get some other agencies involved—maybe even FDLE. Let me think about it and work on it and get back to you."

"Thinks it's too dangerous, don't he?" Blade says.

Sheri walks into the living room from her bedroom and says, "Thinks what is?"

I tell her. As I do, her face fills with concern.

"I think it's a great idea," she says, "but it's just not worth the risk. I'm making peace with everything that happened and with not knowing. If the police find out what happened, fine, but I don't want anything happening to you two or Alana and Ashlynn just to give me answers. I just keep thinking . . . knowing what happened to him isn't going to change whatever that was. Isn't going to bring him back to me. It's not worth the risk of anyone else's life. I mean it. I really am gettin' to a place of peace over it now. Part of what helped me get there was Serge threatening us. I really, really want y'all to quit investigating. I've come to terms with what having answers is really worth and what it's not. And it's not worth y'all taking risks like these. It's just not. I'm okay . . . I really am. And I want y'all to be."

"We're gonna be okay," I say. "We can keep everyone safe and keep tryin' to close this case. As far as the Halloween reenactment . . . Instead of the request coming from any of us, it will come from the sheriff's office. Not from Rick—his name won't even be mentioned—but from the office itself. I think that will help. I've thought about it . . . and . . . I wouldn't do it if I thought it was too much of a risk—especially where you, Ashlynn, and Alana are concerned."

"Well, obviously I can't stop you," she says, "but I'd rather y'all not do it. I have a very bad feeling about it, and the last time

I had a feeling like this and didn't do anything about it, I lost my son."

CHAPTER
FORTY

A FEW DAYS LATER, Rick and I are on the way to have one more go at Brad Reed while Blade is on protection and research duty.

"I think we've nearly got everything set for the Halloween party at Suzi's," he says. "She's been extremely helpful and accommodating. The request came from the sheriff's office, so there shouldn't be any blowback for any of us."

"That's great," I say. "Thanks for taking care of that—and for keeping us all out of it."

"Just hope it works and we figure some things out. Oh, and I didn't tell you, but . . . we took it a step further. This is really cool. So . . . we've told everyone—Suzi, the band, the people that were there that night—that this is all part of a true crime TV show and that a camera crew will be there that night filming. Seeing you and Blade use that on Thompson the other night gave me the idea. We're bringing in FDLE agents to pose as the film crew. And we've let everyone know about the huge Crime Stoppers reward for anyone providing helpful information. So hopefully they'll be motivated to attend and contribute. And check this—Suzi decided on her own to close the bar that night and make this a private by-invitation-only event. Besides a few of us, everyone there will have been there the night it happened."

"Really?" I say. "That's . . . I'm really . . . I'm shocked she'd do that, but that's excellent."

"I had to do some serious fast-talking to the sheriff, call in every favor I was owed, and if anything goes wrong I'll probably be out of a job, but . . . wanted to roll the dice while we have some momentum goin' on this thing."

"I agree, but it's so brave of you to do. I really admire your approach to your job and appreciate you doing all this."

"Don't tell me. Tell Ashlynn."

"I will."

"How are things going with you two?"

"Great, I think. We've been spending a ton of time together—especially since I started helpin' with protection too."

"That's . . . I'm very glad to hear it. Like it when good people find each other."

We ride along in silence for a moment, him with an irrepressible smile on his face.

"You really think Hobo Girl's gonna show?"

"Oh, yeah, I forgot to mention, I got authorization to use some of the reward money for this event, so we're able to overpay Suzi for hosting the private party and overpay the band reuniting and playing. Their broke asses will be there. We're using the lead singer from the band Thompson plays in at the Copacabana. And since it's Halloween she'll be in costume. So for the first time they'll actually have a hobo girl. And, of course, they all think they're going to be on TV."

"You gonna sit in on any songs?" I ask. "We still haven't heard you play?"

"I wish we both could," he says. "But we'll be too busy. But let's jam together after this is all over."

"It's a date."

"I figured we'd also invite people who are connected to the

case but who weren't there that night—like Amanda Woods. Aiden's mom if she wants to be. And Ashlynn'll be working."

Pulling up and parking in front of the Creek County Court-house, we get out and begin looking for Brad Reed. Spotting him on the opposite side beneath a palm tree, we head that way.

He's wearing a dark, expensive-looking suit, a white shirt, a burgundy tie, and has a thin briefcase in his right hand. He's talking to what looks to be a colleague—a young woman with short blond hair in a navy-blue pantsuit holding a briefcase of her own.

By the time we reach them, the two are parting company, and as Brad turns he begins shaking his head.

Rick says, "We were hoping that now you've joined the good guys you might be willing to talk to us."

Brad had recently crossed the aisle and gone from being a high-priced defense attorney to becoming a well-respected prosecutor.

He shakes his head and frowns. "It's that kind of thinking that's the problem. There are good guys on both sides. We have to have a good and rigorous defense for our system to work."

"Yeah, yeah," Rick says. "But that's avoiding the question."

"And who is *us*?" Brad asks.

"This is Lucas Burke," he says. "He's a PI consulting on the case."

"Will you talk to us or not?" Rick asks.

"Have nothing else to add," Brad says. "I've already said all that I know. Don't see the point of saying it again or taking a chance that I might make up something to fill in the gaps of my memory of that night."

Rick starts to say something but Brad continues.

"But I'll tell you this . . . Aiden wasn't the saint everybody's trying to make him out to be, and I'm not the devil."

"We know," I say. "But what specifically do you mean? In what ways was Aiden not a saint?"

"Mostly just women," he says. "He always had a girlfriend.

Never knew him without one. But he also was always looking to hook up. I mean always. You should've seen him that night. It was embarrassing . . . Inserting himself into conversations and situations. Drunkenly attempting to flirt."

"Is that what y'all fought over?" I ask.

"We didn't fight."

"Poor choice of words," I say. "Sorry. The disagreement you had . . ."

"He was disrespecting Amanda even more than usual," he says. "And I didn't like the way he was treating Jade. But only a fool tries to reason with someone who was fucked up as he was."

"Weren't exactly sober yourself, were you?" Rick says.

"Compared to him I was."

"Did he hit on Jade?" Rick asks. "Is that what make you mad?"

"I didn't have anything to do with what happened to him that night," Brad says. "Whatever that was. And I have no idea what it was. Don't know any more about it than y'all do—probably less. And I'm not not talking just to be an asshole. I just have nothing else to say."

"I appreciate that," I say. "But for someone like me . . . new to the case . . . it helps more than you can imagine to hear you tell us what you remember versus us reading it in a report."

"Y'all have any idea how much money I've been offered to tell my story?" Brad says. "I'm not trying to capitalize on this in any way. I wish none of this would've ever happened. It didn't just impact Aiden's life. It's something we all carry. Every new person I meet—every client and coworker—wants to hear about that night. I feel the worst for Amanda and Sheri, but it's been unimaginably difficult on all of us. Y'all don't think I want to find out what happened to him more than anybody?"

"You don't act like it," Rick says.

I wince inside, and wish Rick wouldn't take that tack.

"So because I'm not willing to make shit up and be a part of the circus surrounding this case, I don't want him found?"

"We're not asking you to talk to the media or be a part of anything other than helping us get to the bottom of this thing."

"If I knew anything at all, I would've already told his mom. I just don't."

"Did you actually see him walk over to the band and start talking to them?" I ask.

"I definitely saw him walk in that direction, but I don't really remember him starting to talk to anybody in the band—but I can't really be sure of that at this point. I just don't remember—and I'm not gonna stand here and make shit up trying to prove to y'all that I'm one of the good guys, trying to be helpful."

"And you didn't notice anybody staring at him, stalking him, getting into an argument with him?" I say.

"He pissed off a lot of people that night," he says. "Including me. He was acting like he was . . . like he was on something other than alcohol. So there were plenty of people mad at him, but . . . I didn't see anyone who looked like they'd kill him over it. But I don't know and I've got to go."

"HOW IS EVERYTHING THERE?" I ask.

We're back in the car and I'm on the phone with Blade.

"Borin' as shit, but nobody's dead yet."

"When I get back I'll take a shift and let you get out of there."

"All good," she says. "Just sort of wish Serge would show up so I could blow a big hole in his ass. Well, another one."

"Anything else interesting in the surveillance footage so far."

"Few things. Maybe. Be interested to see what you and Rick think. Got a dark figure on the video that might actually be Aiden,"

"Really?"

"Can't be sure. It's a distant shot from the auto parts place not far from Suzi's. Shows a dark figure walking toward downtown—well after Suzi's closed. If it's Aiden . . . it means he got out of Suzi's that night without being seen. Sheri may be right. Maybe he *is* still alive. Staged all this to start a new life somewhere, posted on his father's funeral page, broke into his mama's house last week. I don't know. Could be."

"That's huge."

"Could be," she says. "Could be nothing. I'll keep going.

Figure I'll try to get through the rest of it and have y'all look at everything I find."

"Sounds good. We just spoke with Brad and—"

"He talked to y'all?" she asks.

"Sort of," I say. "A little."

"What'd he say?"

I start to say something but stop as Rick takes a call.

"What is it?" she asks.

"Hold on one second."

"Got nothin' better to do," she says.

A few minutes later, when I return to Blade I say, "Rick thinks he's got a line on Sebastian. We're gonna go check it out. I'll hit you up when we—"

"Be careful."

"Y'all too."

FORTY-TWO

JAI ALAI, a variation of basque pelota, is a sport involving a ball that is bounced off a walled-in area with a hand-held narrow wicker basket known as a *cesta*. The sport is mostly played and is most popular in Spain, the south west of France, and Latin American countries.

In the United States, jai alai enjoyed some popularity as a gambling alternative to horse and greyhound racing, and remains popular in parts of Florida, where it's used as a basis for pari-mutuel or pool betting.

Forgotten Coast Jai Alai, North Florida's only jai alai facility, opened in 1978, and from the very beginning was plagued with problems.

Not long before the grand opening, one of the co-owners died of a massive heart attack. His estate, valued at $32 million, was disputed by his heirs, relatives, business associates, and others in multiple court cases that dragged on for more than thirteen years. An attorney involved in one of the cases said, "There are all sorts of wild allegations on the record: suitcases of gems, hidden gold, chicanery, injustice, but nothing was ever proven."

In 1988 the players of Forgotten Coast Jai Alai joined other striking players and walked out over contract disputes. The sport itself was prone to player injuries—cuts and concussions and the like—and of course, the betting component led to increased organized crime activity. However, the decline of the game's popularity in Florida, which began in the 1980s, was mostly the result of changes in state laws and the increased availability of gambling options.

For over three decades, the Forgotten Coast Jai Alai building has been empty, abandoned, experiencing the slow death of decay, the huge facility now known primarily for two things—an enormous infestation of bats and the sometime squat of the mentally ill with nowhere else to go.

As Rick and I were pulling away from the courthouse, Rick received a call from a narcotics investigator who had gotten a tip from one of his CIs that Sebastian Lewinsky is living rough in the abandoned Forgotten Coast Jai Alai building.

Weeds grow through the cracks in the parking lot and vines cover large swaths of the huge, dilapidated building.

"Here," Rick says, as he reaches into the back seat and hands me a large metal flashlight.

We follow neon graffiti that wraps around the side of the building and into a set of side doors mostly missing the glass that was once in them.

Stepping over and ducking under the shards of glass, We slip into a room of overturned tables and a tile floor covered with betting tickets.

"Want to make a wager?" I ask.

"On?"

"Whether or not he's in here."

"Should probably make it on whether or not we find him even if he is. This place is bigger than I remember."

Clicking on our flashlights, we pass beneath a bird nest in an exit sign and into a long, dark, narrow corridor.

The foul, fetid smell in the air is overwhelming, and I try to breathe through my mouth to avoid smelling it.

The corridor is littered with more tickets and trash, an old-fashioned rotary-dial wall phone, and a hand truck. It opens onto a massive lobby with an escalator at one end.

Old windows and holes in the walls and ceiling let a small amount of the late-afternoon sunlight stream into the huge, open area.

Beneath their feet, the soiled carpet is wet and spongy and littered with trash.

Long counters run the length of each wall—one side for concession, the other for betting. An open door behind the betting counter reveals a bank room, its floor littered with empty coin roll wrappers, beyond which is an enormous wall safe.

We maneuver around the charred remains of campfires, broken glass crunching beneath our feet.

On the far wall beyond the escalator, a row of makeshift tents and cardboard houses have been propped up.

"Creek County Sheriff's Investigator," Rick says. "Step out slowly with your hands up and identify yourself."

Two huge black hands slowly poke out from one of the tents.

"Don't shoot, damn it. I'm comin' out. Don't shoot me, you son of a bitch."

"I'm not going to shoot you," Rick says. "What's your name?"

"Henry," he says. "Hank."

Henry Hank is a giant with a huge, unkempt fro and a long, curly black beard, and is in a raincoat and unlaced army boots. And nothing else. The open raincoat reveals a soft, hairy belly, beneath which is a huge, unerect phallus hanging to the left.

"Henry Hank is a show-er not a grower," Rick says.

"*Hey*," Henry Hank yells. "Y'all really come here to talk about my big dick?"

"Sorry," Rick says. "But I mean . . . my God. Anyway, we're looking for a guy. Sebastian Lewinsky."

"Seabass, yeah," he says, nodding. "Lives upstairs. But, man, I wouldn't go up there I's you. Bad shit happens up there."

"Anybody else up there?"

"Man, I don't know. Peoples comes and go from this place all the time. I can't keep up. Can I get back to my knitting now?"

"Sure. And thanks for your help."

"Don't mention it. And don't feel bad for gawking at my big donkey dick. Er'body do."

The big man disappears back into the tent that appears far too small to hold him.

Rick moves over to the escalator and I follow.

Before beginning to climb the steps of the still escalator, he turns and scans the area, his eyes following the moving beam of his flashlight.

"Ready?" he asks.

I nod.

"I'm going to be looking mostly forward, scanning right and left," Rick says. "Will you keep an eye on what's behind us?"

"Sure."

We begin to slowly climb the metal and rubber stairs, maneuvering around a series of old, large monitors, their glass screens broken, their electronic guts hanging out.

"Creek County Sheriff's Investigator," Rick yells. "We're here to speak with Sebastian Lewinsky. All we want to do is talk to you. You're not in trouble. Not under arrest. Just a quick talk and then we're gone."

As we make the ascent, we begin to hear the enormous cloud of bats from the darkness above, their fluttering wings and the high-pitched chirps and clicks of their echolocation process.

We reach the top floor to find an open space and what were once booze and concession stands. More trash on the floor. More dust on everything. More graffiti on the walls.

Making our way over to the arena, we look in, down the rows and rows of seats to the court below that is littered with trash and containing a single jai alai ball.

Above us the immense black ceiling is moving.

Shining our lights upward, we see what appears to be millions of bats blotting out the ceiling.

"That has to be one of the largest colonies of bats in the world," Rick says.

He turns and I turn with him.

After identifying himself again, he says, "Sebastian? Are you up here? We just want to talk."

No answer comes back from the void—only the sounds of bats from the black, undulating sea above.

"Doesn't seem like anyone's here," Rick says. "But let's look around a little."

We move behind a concession counter and into a huge commercial kitchen. Most of the appliances have been removed, leaving behind a tangle of exposed wires and pipes.

Sections of the sheetrock walls are missing, revealing the metal frame beneath and the room beyond.

The floors are littered with trash and evidence of campfires and makeshift beds.

More graffiti, thick dust, and cobwebs, but also the smell of mildew.

I sense we're being watched, but when I scan the area with my light no one is there.

I follow Rick down another corridor, off of which are rooms that look to have once been apartments for players, many of them still containing mattresses—most of which are now on the floor and soiled beyond what it seems a human being could be capable of.

Occasionally, a bat flutters by us, but for the most part the creatures are not in this section of the building.

Eventually, we arrive back in the second floor lobby close to where we began.

The bats are louder out here, and though most are in the arena, there are plenty out here as well.

We cross the open area, around and in between overturned tables and chairs, a growing stench assaulting our nostrils.

"That's the unmistakable stench of—"

"Death," Rick says as he withdraws his weapon.

We reach an open elevator shaft on the far wall and look down into its deep, narrow abyss to see several dead bodies in various stages of decay inside.

The sickening smell along with the shock of the horrific sight makes me dizzy and I nearly pitch forward into the shaft.

Rick grabs me and the two of us back away from the terrifying tableau.

"You okay?" Rick asks.

"Yeah. Sorry about that. Just got light-headed. Thanks for—"

"Don't mention it. Let's get out of here. I'm gonna call for backup and the FDLE crime scene unit. We'll secure the place and start processing the scene. If Sebastian is here—"

A dark figure pounces out of the darkness, knocking us down.

Our flashlights fall and roll a few feet away, shining back on us, illuminating a small circle of light on the floor beneath the vast, dark void.

I turn to see what might be an older, long-haired, long-bearded filthy version of Sebastian Lewinsky on top of Rick.

I push up and spin around to help.

At first I think Sebastian is punching Rick, but then a glint of light reveals he has a blade in his hand and is stabbing Rick repeatedly in a fevered frenzy of surreal proportions.

I jump up and kick the man off of Rick, whose clothes are already wet with blood.

The instant Sebastian hits the floor, he rolls, spins, and turns back toward me, readying himself to lunge back at us to continue his assault.

As he does, Rick, with what seems to be the last remaining life force inside him, raises his weapon and fires two rounds that explode in Sebastian's chest.

The sound is deafening in the darkness and the colony of bats grows louder and begins to swarm around them.

Rick's hand falls to the ground with the gun still in it as I move over to him, futilely attempting to stop the bleeding while trying to tap 911 into my phone.

CHAPTER
FORTY-THREE

"WHO THE HELL ARE YOU AGAIN?" the sheriff is asking.

Hands cuffed behind me, Rick's blood on my clothes, I am standing beside the back of the patrol car I have just been pulled from.

The patrol car is one of many emergency service vehicles out in front of the crumbling Forgotten Coast Jai Alai building.

It had rained earlier and the air is dense with dampness, the waxed vehicles around me beaded by a thousand tiny raindrops.

"Lucas Burke," I say.

I can't believe this is what is going to send me back to prison —assisting a law enforcement officer, not killing Dimitri, not being set up by Logan Owens, but actually working with the good guys.

"I know your damn name," Rigsby says. "I want to know just what the hell you were doing here with my investigator and your part in his death."

"He's dead?"

Sheriff Ford Rigsby is both old and old school. Beneath his gray crewcut, his sunburned skin is thick, deeply lined, and leathery. He's a tall, large white man with long arms and thick, scarred hands and misshapen fingers, the joints of which are swollen and deformed.

"Let me explain how this particular type of conversation works," he says. "I'm in charge of the questions. You're in charge of the answers. Stay in your lane and answer my questions. Don't ask me questions of your own."

I briefly explain my connection to Sheri and the case and my qualifications for looking into the assault on Sheri and Aiden's disappearance. "I've been unofficially assisting Rick with—"

"Hold on there just a damn minute," Rigsby interrupts. "Unless you want to be charged with his murder and hindering a police investigation, you haven't been assisting anybody in my department, unofficially or otherwise. Understand?"

I nod.

"I don't know what the hell Carson was thinkin' . . . Guess he wasn't, which is what got him killed, but if I hear you say anything like that again I swear to you I will charge you with his murder—and I can make it stick. Understand?"

I nod.

"Ask yourself," Rigsby continues, "do you want to go to jail or home tonight?"

The thought of being able to go home tonight, back to Alana and Blade and Ashlynn makes my eyes sting.

"And I better not hear that you're investigating our case anymore either," he says. "You're a convicted felon, not a PI. You're a scammer. A joke. Not qualified for shit. See him?"

Rigsby points to a casually dressed thirty-something man across the way speaking into a digital recorder.

"He's a reporter," Rigsby continues. "He's also my sister's kid. He'll pretty much print whatever I tell him to. Do you have any idea how much misery I can rain down on you with just one story? Enough to make you wish it had been you instead of Carson."

CHAPTER
FORTY-FOUR

"ARE YOU OKAY?" Blade asks.

She had hugged me when I first walked in and now has smears of Rick's blood on her clothes.

I nod.

Bleary-eyed, raw-bone weary, I feel empty, depleted in every way—emotionally, mentally, spiritually, and physically.

"Still in shock," I say, "but I'm not so numb I can't feel guilt."

"What happened ain't your fault."

"Where is Ashlynn?" I ask. "I've got to tell her."

"Who else got killed?" she asks.

"Sebastian," I say. "He was—"

"No, besides him," she says. "You said *two* people."

"Just Sebastian and Rick, not counting all the previous victims in the elevator shaft."

"When did Rick die?" she asks.

I'm confused, wonder why she's asking. "This afternoon," I say. "Not sure exactly when. Had to be sometime between the EMTs arriving and when I spoke to Ford Rigsby."

"No," she says. "Rick's not dead. The news said he's in critical condition following surgery, but he's not dead."

Had Rigsby meant he was as good as dead or was he lying to

me to increase and intensify the threats he was making?

"Outlook's not great, but he's still alive. He might make it."

"You sure?"

"Yeah. Ashlynn's at the hospital now."

"The sheriff told me he was dead," I say. "Said he could charge me as an accessory to his murder."

"He was fuckin' with you. He knows if you hadn't been there Rick's dead ass would be down that elevator shaft. You saved his life. Sheriff won't ever acknowledge that."

"Good," I say. "I was never there."

She nods, understanding everything I've done, everything I'm doing is a violation of my probation.

"It's too bad you weren't there to knock Sebastian off Rick and call an ambulance. It's a fuckin' tragedy that you weren't there to apply pressure to his wounds until the EMTs got there. If you had . . . every second of life he gets from here on out is thanks to you."

"I hope he'll pull through and survive," I say.

"Thanks to you he's getting the chance. Feel better now?"

I nod. "Much."

"I know what you wantin' to do, but I want to show you something first."

"What is it I'm wanting to do?" I ask.

"Wake Alana up and hug her."

I laugh. "You're not wrong."

"I been watchin' the surveillance footage and . . . tomorrow is Halloween. It's now or never. And I think I discovered footage from inside Suzi's that's been altered and maybe a shot of Aiden actually outside of the bar later that night. The image caught by a security camera from the parts place on the corner I was tellin' you about."

"Well, no matter what happened that night or how he got out the bar," I say. "There's a good chance we know where he wound up."

She nods. "It the bottom of that elevator shaft."

CHAPTER
FORTY-FIVE

I DROP my bloody clothes into the trash can instead of the hamper, wondering if Rick will survive, and if he does what the lasting physical and psychological damage will look like.

Pausing for a moment, I take a deep breath, then turn on the shower.

As I do, I catch a glimpse of myself in the mirror.

The figure in the reflection looks pale and exhausted and in shock, and not recognizable as me.

I am numb and everything, including myself seems a great distance away.

After a few moments, I stumble into the shower.

Making the water as hot as I can stand it, I barely notice the sting on my reddening skin as it sluices down my weary body.

I think about what happened, the events replaying in my mind as if I'm witnessing what happened to someone else.

I feel a disassociation from what happened and my part in it, and yet I wonder what I could've done differently.

While cuffed and in the custody of the Creek County Sheriff, I had heard the sheriff and other investigators talking about Lewinsky.

He had experienced a psychotic break and the onset of schizophrenia sometime near when Aiden disappeared. After being diagnosed and undergoing some inpatient treatment, he had broken out of the facility and disappeared. Off his meds since then, he had been living rough and evidently growing increasingly violent. They theorized that Aiden may have been his first victim but certainly wasn't his last.

They further theorized that the rotting bodies in the elevator shaft were most likely those of other homeless people who had come to the abandoned building looking for a place to live.

I stay in the shower until all the hot water is gone—and for a while after that, barely noticing the icy needles poking into the blood-reddened surface of my canned-ham skin.

When I finally get out of the shower, I towel off slightly and fall into the bed still damp, lacking the energy and the will to do anything—even get under the covers.

I court sleep but it won't come.

So I think.

What if Sebastian had nothing to do with what happened to Aiden?

What if his psychotic break is unrelated to Aiden's disappearance?

It's at least possible. Has to be considered.

Or what if his break is related to Aiden's disappearance—but only indirectly? He could've witnessed something rather than done it.

Tomorrow is Halloween. Time is running out. What will happen to the re-enactment now that Rick is fighting for his life? Will the other cops still be at Suzi's tomorrow night?

With all the original people there on Halloween, I can't help but believe that more facts will come out, more truths be revealed, more suspects identified, more insights gained—and we can't let that opportunity slip by. A closed party at Suzi's with the people who were there that night and Hobo Girl playing isn't ever going to happen again.

Blade slips into the room and climbs into the twin bed across from mine.

"You asleep?" she whispers.

"May never sleep again."

"Don't be such a pussy."

I laugh out loud in the darkness.

"Got an update on Rick," she says. "He's critical, but stable. He makes it through the night . . . he's got a good chance of making it."

"Good," I say. "That's good news."

"He's gonna make it," she says. "I can feel it."

Her certainty makes me feel more confident. She's not known for excessive hopeful optimism.

I say, "If Sebastian is schizophrenic . . . psychotic . . . or whatever . . . I can't see him being able to make Aiden vanish so thoroughly. I think it would be like his frenzied attack on Rick and he wouldn't care about hiding his body—or even be able to."

"Could've done it before havin' his psychotic break or . . . what if he killed him and really wasn't concerned about his body not being found, but because of where or how he killed him it worked out that way. Could've killed him next to the bay and rolled his body into it and the bay did the rest. Could've killed him in the construction site and fresh concrete did the rest. Him being the doer and Aiden's body never bein' found could be almost unrelated."

"True."

"Think they'll still do the party and the operation tonight?" she asks.

"Not sure who to ask."

"We still goin' either way, right?"

"Oh, hell yeah," I say, starting to feel a little more like myself. "And I may have an idea about how to deal with Serge."

CHAPTER
FORTY-SIX

AS IF A REPLICA of that Halloween night two years ago, it's raining—an odd, light rain that refracts the pale, anemic points of light scattered throughout the dark, haunted night in irregular and surreal ways.

More thick mist than light rain, the effect is a hazy, hypnotic vibe, translucent and tremulous.

Suzi's is lit mostly by candelabras and jack-o-lanterns, the flicker of the flames in the darkness creating a strobe-like effect that resembles an early Lumière brothers' short film.

Hobo Girl is playing Eurythmics' "Here Comes the Rain Again."

Blade is dressed as Suzanne "Crazy Eyes" Warren from *Orange is the New Black*, the sleeves of a too-big gray sweatshirt coming out of her brown inmate uniform, multiple short, small dreads rising from her head.

I'm dressed as Woody from *Toy Story*, which allows me not only to hide a knife in one of my boots but carry an actual loaded revolver in the holster on my belt. The firearm is a replica of an old cowboy six-shooter and looks like a prop, which is what I'm counting on everyone to believe.

If I use either weapon I'll be sent back to prison, so I hope I won't need to, but I'd rather go to prison than the cemetery—or have something happen to Blade or Ashlynn.

Blade and I both have drinks in our hands, but neither of us are drinking.

As we look around at the crowd, Hobo Girl plays "I'm Only Happy When It Rains" by Garbage, and like with the previous song, it helps to have a female front man, and they've never sounded better.

Scanning the room, I try to pick out the undercover police, but can't be sure of any besides the fake camera crew.

When I see Serge across the room talking to Suzi, I look around and locate Bobby Doll. Catching his eye, I nod toward Serge. Bobby Doll smiles and nods.

Bobby Doll isn't much to look at—a small white twenty-something with pale skin, disconcerting green eyes, and a buzzcut he does himself—but he's a truly dangerous individual with sociopathic tendencies who is very good with a gun and enjoys using it like no one I've ever seen. Blade and I had helped him out more than a few times when we were all kids in the system, and there's nothing he won't do for us. We called him in for extra firepower tonight, and we're just hoping he won't make too big a mess of Serge and any other bad guys we might encounter.

Serge is dressed as Tony Montana from *Scarface* and Suzi is dressed in drag as Norman Bates in his mother's dress—complete with wig and kitchen knife.

When Serge spots me and Blade, he leaves Suzi mid-sentence and heads toward us.

By the time he reaches us, Bobby Doll, who is dressed as John Doe from *Seven*, complete with blood-spattered white shirt-sleeve shirt and bloodied-bandaged fingertips, is standing beside us.

As Serge walks up, Blade says, "No, we don't want to say hello to your little friend."

"You guys," Serge says. "What am I gonna do with you? I

gave you fair warning, no? I don't get it. Why you not listen to your new pal, Serge, huh?"

"You got time to walk us through your movements on the night of Aiden's disappearance?" I ask.

Serge stops, shakes his head, and considers me for a long moment. Laughing, as if genuinely amused, he says, "Okay, cowboy, have it your way. Serge didn't want anything bad to happen to you and your, aw, prison dyke, but . . . What can I do? It's a lesson I have to learn—letting go. I can't take responsibility for other people. Serge must learn this, no? 'God grant me serenity to accept things I cannot change, the courage to change things I can, and the wisdom to know the difference that is between them.' Serge accepts he cannot make you value a long, safe life. I hope you have accepted the fate of the choice you have made."

"Accept this—" I say. "The police are aware of your threats against us and our families. If anything happens to us . . . they would take you down, but—"

"They can't even keep themselves from getting hacked up like Thanksgiving turkey, no?"

"They would take you down," I repeat, "if they could, but . . . they won't be able to."

"Exactly," Serge says. "This is exactly right my friend."

"They won't be able to . . ." I say, "because there won't be anything left of you to take down. That's because our friend, John Doe here, will, after a particularly brutal and lengthy torture session, obliterate you off the face of the fuckin' earth as if you had never been born."

Serge looks at Bobby Doll for the first time.

"The hell are you?" Serge asks him.

"Me? Just your garden variety sociopath with homicidal tendencies."

Blade says, "Just between us . . . that's not fake blood on his shirt."

There is a palpable change in Serge. He swallows before

speaking and his words have the tinny, hollow quality of a bad actor. "If you think Serge can be scared off, man, you—"

"Yeah, yeah," Bobby Doll says. "Say your lines so you don't lose face, but . . . we all know you know the real from the fake news. And while we knowin' shit, know this . . . Just in case that little gin-soaked, titty-bar brain of yours thinks sneaking up and back-shooting me will solve your problems, not only do I have eyes in the back of my head, but I have brothers and other family members a hell of a lot meaner than I am that will keep you alive wishing you were dead, begging for your death, a lot longer than I would have."

Serge starts to say something, but Bobby Doll holds up his blood-covered hand. "Let's be done with this shit. You're beginning to bore me and I may have to eighty-six a bitch right here right now in the middle of this perfect little party. Run along now. And from this moment forward, pray to whatever god you pray to that nothin' happens to these two or their families, because if something does—no matter what or who might be responsible—you know what that means for you."

FORTY-SEVEN

"IT'S SO strange to be back," Jade is saying. She is one of a handful of people not in costume. "Haven't been since that night."

Blade and I are standing with Jade near the end of the mostly empty bar.

Behind the bar, Suzi is talking to Ashlynn and the barback. Instead of a kid, the barback is a late-twenties man with pale skin, fine blond hair, and blue eyes so light they almost seem colorless.

"Does being here trigger any memories?" Blade asks.

"Sure. Of course."

"Any that you had forgotten about until now?"

She shrugs. "Maybe. I just remember Aiden being so . . . agitated. He couldn't be still. It was like he was hyperactive or something. He kept rubbing and itching his skin like he was having an allergic reaction to something. And . . . he couldn't let anything go. I mean . . . Brad can be a jerk. Trust me, I know. But that night . . . Aiden was looking for a fight. Everything bothered him. He took everything the wrong way."

Amanda Woods, in a small, sexy Little Red Riding Hood costume, rushes over to us.

"I've just remembered something," she says. "I know I wasn't here that night, but . . . somehow it helps to be here. I'm . . . it's unlocking things. I remember this thing Aiden said because that song was playing while we were on the phone."

All three of us turn to look at the band.

Hobo Girl is playing Willie Nelson's "Blue Eyes Crying in the Rain."

"He said a lot of things that didn't make sense that night," she says. "Like I said . . . he was out of it. Exhausted from not sleeping, staying up all week studying, the stress and pressure of his exams. He was strung out on something and drunk. It was hard to hear him when he was in here and he was mumbling and slurring his words. I remember he said something about dropping out of school and joining the band. He was always talking about that—being in a band instead of becoming a doctor. I said something like "You can't do that" or something, and he said, "I may not have a choice." I asked what he meant and he just said we'd talk about it later. He hung up and I never . . . It was the last time I spoke to him. But . . . something in the way he said he might not have a choice . . . Not sure what that meant, but . . . it sounded like he really believed it—that something he had done or . . . something was going to force him to drop out of medical school."

"And you got no idea what he was talkin' about?" Blade asks.

"None at all," she says. "Before, he always talked about wanting to be in a band. And sometimes he'd say he'd rather do that than be a doctor. Even said he planned to start a band after medical school, but it was always partially playful. And he never mentioned not finishing school—and especially not having a choice about it."

"You can't think of any reason why he'd say something like that?" I ask. "What he may have meant?"

She shakes her head. "None. Sorry. And it may be nothing, but . . . I don't know. It sounded like something. Anyway . . . just wanted to let you know. I'm gonna walk around some more and see if I remember anything else."

Blade nudges me with her elbow and points to the door.

I turn to see Sheri, dressed as what I believe to be one of the Golden Girls, walking into the bar.

I had explained to her how potentially upsetting and even dangerous tonight could be, and she had agreed not to come. She was supposed to take Alana trick-or-treating, then to a carnival at the rec center, and yet here she is.

I walk over to her and Blade follows.

"Wasn't expecting to see you here," I say when we reach her.

"Couldn't stay away. Had to see it all for myself. I won't get in the way. I promise."

"Where is Alana?"

"With Robin and that nice deputy. Told I wouldn't be long. Y'all just go back to what you were doing. Don't mind me."

"Would you like a drink?" I ask.

She nods.

"I'll go grab it. Blade'll help you find a good spot to sit."

I look at Sheri. "Is there any reason why Aiden may have had to drop out of school?"

"What do you mean?"

"Did he ever mention anything about not having a choice about whether he kept attending medical school? Grades? Money? Some kind of trouble?"

She shakes her head. "No. Why? As far as I know everything was fine with school and he was doing well. Surely you don't think what happened to him has anything to do with school, do you?"

FORTY-EIGHT

WHEN HOBO GIRL goes on break, dance versions of Halloween music is pumped through the house system.

I approach the stage to talk to the band while Blade talks to the two young women who had been seen on the surveillance footage with Aiden outside the bar not long before it closed.

The members of Hobo Girl are dressed as iconic band members—just not from the same band. Among them are members of Kiss, the Village People, The Beatles, and The Stones.

"It's so trippy to be back," Terrick Bushnell is saying. Beneath his black rock hair wig, his face is painted white with a black star around his right eye and very red lips. "Never thought we'd play together again—let alone here on *Hallofreakinween*. What the hell, man?"

"Still can't believe that shit about Seabass," Sammy Chastain says. He's dressed as Ringo Starr circa 1969. "It's weird not having him here playing with us."

"What's *weird* . . . is that he lost his freakin' marbles and offed a bunch of people."

Thompson Tait is standing there with them, dressed as the

construction worker from the Village People, and appears disinterested and sullen.

Sammy says, "You think if he hadn't killed that Aiden dude and disappeared that night, he might have killed us?"

"Think he may have tried," Terrick says.

"Oh," Thompson says, adding to the conversation for the first time, "'cause you're such a badass and could've—"

"Nah, man, that's not how I meant it. I just meant he might have tried. That's all. Not that we could've stopped him if he did."

"He wasn't a big dude," Thompson says. "Hard time seeing him overpower Shaw."

Sammy says, "All it takes is one surprise blow to the head or stab to a major blood vessel or organ and . . . the biggest, strongest bastard on the planet will be incapacitated."

"Hey, man," Terrick says to me, "I remembered something while we were playing tonight I had forgotten. He got into it with the bouncer. Shaw, I mean. He was over by the bar talkin' to the owner, Suzi, and—it didn't look like a friendly conversation by the way—and the Russian or Ukrainian or whatever he is guy came up and got in his face. Suzi walked away—went into the back I think. Not sure. And Shaw just kind of collapsed onto a barstool."

"I missed all that," Sammy says, "but at one point I saw Jasper try to come around and help him and Serge stopped him . . . kind of warned him off."

"Jasper?"

"Tollis. The barback."

I turn and look at the almost albino barback.

"What happened then?" I ask as I look back toward them.

"Nothin'," Terrick says. "Was near the end of the night. Didn't really pay attention to him. Next time he was on my radar is when his drunk ass was stumbling around our equipment."

Thompson says, "Then he made the fatal mistake of following Seabass into the back."

As I thank them and move off to talk to Jasper Tollis, Thompson follows me.

"Hey," he says when we are out of earshot of the other band members. "Them catching Sebastian isn't going to change my TV deal any, is it?"

"It shouldn't," I say. "But it'd help if you think of any other details you can share. I don't mean make anything up. I mean anything you may have held back or anything that you remember because of tonight."

JASPER TOLLIS'S personality is as anemic as his pale appearance.

Though he's in his late twenties, he acts as if he's a prepubescent boy, and implicit in every word and action he takes is an unspoken apology.

"You were working the night Aiden Shaw disappeared, weren't you?" I ask.

Blade is back with me.

The only thing she had been able to get out of the two young women Aiden had been speaking to out front the night he disappeared was that he was most definitely hitting on them and he walked back into the bar as they left.

Tollis nods.

"What were Suzi and Aiden and Serge arguing about?" I ask.

He shrugs.

"You don't know or you won't say?" Blade asks.

He doesn't respond.

Hobo Girl takes the stage again and opens its next set with a punk version of "Have You Ever Seen the Rain."

"What made Aiden fall down onto the barstool?" I ask.

He shrugs again. "Just didn't feel good I guess. I don't know.

Everybody always drinks more than they realize. Maybe. I'm sorry, but I don't know."

"When you tried to check on him or help him, why did Serge stop you?"

"I try to help people," he says. "They come in here for a good time. I just want to make sure they have one and are okay. That's all. But sometimes Mr. Serge has to deal with them his way and it's not my place to say or do anything. I don't know. I like my job. I like the music and the people having a good time. That's all. I want to keep my job. Don't want to make anybody upset at me. Miss Suzi's so good to me. Like my big sister. Mr. Serge's all right. He just wants people to behave themselves and . . . He's never been bad to me."

"It's okay," Ashlynn says coming up to us. "You're okay, Jasper. You're not in trouble. They're just trying to find out what happened to Aiden Shaw."

"Yes, ma'am."

"Can you think of anything that could help them figure out what happened to Aiden that night?"

"No, ma'am," he says. "I have no idea. I'd tell you if I did. I swear."

"Okay. It's okay. Go get us two more cases of Coors Light."

He nods rapidly and says, "Yes, ma'am."

As he rushes away, Hobo Girl starts "Purple Rain."

Ashlynn says, "He's a good kid. Sort of slow and simple, but mostly just shy, quiet, and awkward. Absolute heart of gold. Do anything he can for anybody. Lend them money for more drinks or a cab or even give them a ride home. He gets nervous talking to people—especially when he thinks he might get in trouble for something."

Blade says. "We were told on the night Aiden disappeared he stumbled onto a barstool and Jasper tried to help him, but Serge stopped him."

"Wish I had been here," she says. "If you talk to Serge about it . . . please keep Jasper out of it if you can."

"We will," I say. "What do the staff think happened? Where do they think Aiden is?"

"Somewhere in here," she says. "I sometimes catch them searching for him in the walls and attic and shit. Maybe they're right. It's a big building and he hasn't turned up anywhere else. There was that construction going on. His remains could be in a wall or beneath concrete or in some crawlspace."

"But they've all been thoroughly searched," I say.

She shrugs. "I guess. I know they brought some dogs in and looked around, but . . . I guess they could've missed him. They say nobody searched the building more thoroughly than his girl-friend . . . Amanda. Far as I know she's the only one who searched for him that night and several times since then."

"Which night?" I ask.

"Two years ago tonight," she says. "Night it happened. I mean, it wasn't like she was searching for a missing person. She just showed up looking for her boyfriend, but . . . no one else even started looking for him until a few days after that."

CHAPTER
FIFTY

"YOU DIDN'T TELL us you were here the night Aiden went missing," I say.

Amanda looks startled and is unable to speak for a moment. Little Red Riding Hood freezing as if in fear of the Big Bad Wolf. Eventually, she tries to say something, then shakes her head, swallows, and clears her throat. "I wasn't."

"You were seen," Blade says. "We have witnesses."

"I wasn't here when Aiden was here that night," she says. "I wasn't part of anything that went on. I came later. I just . . . I got worried about him. He didn't sound right on the phone and then he stopped answering my calls or responding to my texts. By the time I decided to come check on him it was too late to . . . I didn't get here until after they had closed. There were only a few staff members around, cleaning up, hanging out. They said everyone had already left but I could look around real quick if I wanted to."

"And did you?" Blade asks.

"A little, yeah. Not for long."

"Where all did you look?"

"Everywhere," she says. "Well, everywhere I could. But it was just a quick, cursory glance through the place. I had no idea he was really missing and . . . would never be seen again. I was just making sure my boyfriend was okay. To be honest . . . I figured I'd find him passed out somewhere or having sex with somebody he hooked up with from the bar. I knew they weren't going to let me look for long, so I just sort of ran through everywhere I could."

"Where all did you look?" Blade asks again.

"Everywhere—the construction site, backstage, the elevator, the loading dock. Be easier to tell you where I didn't look."

"Where didn't you look?" I ask.

"I didn't check any kind of attic space or locked storage closets," she says. "And even though I checked the restrooms—male and female—I didn't check every stall. I'm sure I missed other rooms or spaces I don't even know about, but I looked everywhere I could as fast as I could and he wasn't here."

"What time was this?"

"I'm not sure exactly. Probably . . . pushing three. I stopped by the house on the way here. Woke poor Phil up. Think I scared the life out of him. Always wondered if that contributed to his death . . . If his heart was weak and . . . Did I make it weaker? Anyway, I didn't expect anyone to still be here by the time I got here, but there were, and they let me look around."

"Who is *they*?" Blade asks.

"Bartender and a waitress," she says. "Were the only people I saw. I heard a few others, but—"

"*Heard*?" I says. "How? Where?"

"Oh, just in the owner's office," she says. "Backstage. I think that's where they were coming from. There were two locked doors back there. I guess it could've been from either one, but . . . I was told later that one was a storage room, so . . . I was about to knock on both when the bartender appeared at the other end of the hallway and said time was up and we had to go. I wish now that I had insisted on seeing who was behind those doors, but . . . like I said . . . at the time I didn't think he was missing—not in the sense that he really was."

APPROACHING SUZI'S OFFICE, Blade says, "Wish Rick was here. Make this a little more official."

"Yeah," I say, "me too."

"Never thought I'd actually want a cop somewhere."

The band sounds different back here—muted as if playing in a mattress factory—but their version of "A Hard Rain's A-Gonna Fall" is unique and interesting, the female vocals inspired.

"Safe money is Serge is in there with her," she says.

"Should I get Doll to join us?"

"Can't really see a downside to it."

I pull out my phone and text Bobby Doll as we continue.

Just before we reach Suzi's office door, it opens.

Serge gives us a big smile and says, "Come on in, my fine friends."

We step inside to find Suzi, still in her Norman Bates costume, sitting at her desk, a bottle of Jack and a lowball glass in front of her.

"You saw us approaching because of the security cameras in the hall," Blade says. "Wonder why they didn't pick up Aiden that night."

I say, "Witnesses say he followed Sebastian backstage, but he's never seen on the footage. Sebastian is, but not Aiden."

I think how strange this must all look—Woody and Crazy Eyes questioning Norman Bates while Tony Montana observes.

"Clearly the crazy man killed him," Serge says.

"Doesn't explain why he's not on the surveillance footage."

Suzi says, "There's a blind spot—the little area right behind the stage and the hallway. Must've done it there."

"So you see, my good friends," Serge says, "the case it is closed. Have a good day. Bye-bye now."

"I know you doctored the footage," Blade says. "I've got the clip on my phone. See?" She taps a few buttons on her phone then holds it up. "You have to really be looking for it. It's good work, but it's there. Just the faintest flicker where empty hallway footage was inserted over the footage of Aiden back here. The question is . . . Why would you do that? Surely you wouldn't doctor the footage to protect Sebastian? Got no loyalty to him. Guess you could've done it to protect your business—remove the footage of Sebastian killing Aiden for the sake of your business, but . . . My guess is you did it for the only reason you would do it—to protect yourself."

"When Aiden came back here, it wasn't to talk guitars with Sebastian," I say. "He came to see you, didn't he?"

Suzi lets out a laugh, but it sounds forced and hollow. "You see a little static on your phone and you start accusing me of . . . what exactly? That's slander and I can sue your ass."

Her empty threat is made all the more absurd by the costume she's wearing.

I say, "Y'all argued out in the bar and he came back here to finish it."

"You can call it static on my phone if you want to," Blade says, "but I've watched it a few dozen times on a huge high-contrast monitor, and it's an edit, not static or a glitch. There's another one a little later too. You covered up what happened in that hallway, but it doesn't matter what I see. It matters what the FLDE crime lab techs will see."

"What were you arguing about?" I ask.

"Listen to me, my man," Serge says. "There was no argument. The guy was trashed. Wasted. Not making any sense."

"Tell you what," I say, "you tell us what he said and we'll decide for ourselves if it makes sense or not."

"Tell *you* what," he says, "I'll shoot you in the face and you decide if it hurts or not."

"That'd be a brilliant fuckin' way to convince us y'all had nothing to do with Aiden's disappearance," Blade says.

"And genius move given all the cops around," I says.

Suzi nods toward the monitor hanging on the wall across from her desk. We turn to see Bobby Doll approaching the office door, his weapon drawn and down by his side.

"Jesus, man," Serge says, "Guy gives me the creeps." He turns back to Suzi. "You want I should pop them all?"

"No, of course not," she says, shaking her head.

On the monitor, Bobby Doll can be seen standing to the side of the door, his weapon up and ready. The sound of the knock arrives a split second before the monitor shows him knocking.

"I'm not gonna have a shootout at my place of business," Suzi says. She looks up at me. "Call your man and tell him to holster his weapon and stand down. Tell him we're about to open the door very slowly and Serge is going to join him in the hallway while the three of us talk for a minute."

I do as she says. As soon as Doll has his weapon holstered, she opens the door.

"Everything's fine here," Suzi says. "I'm going to talk to these two while you two wait in the hallway—with your mouths shut and your guns holstered. I mean it. I don't want a scene of any kind. Understand? All we'll be doing in here is talking. All you'll being doing out there is waiting—silently. Understand?"

WHEN THE TWO men are in the hallway and door closes behind them, Suzi says, "If I can prove to you that I had nothing to do with Aiden's disappearance, would you agree not to involve the police?"

If Blade is right and the figure she saw on the security footage from the store on the corner is Aiden, then Suzi didn't have anything to do with what happened to him.

We nod.

"I want to hear you say it," Suzi says. "Both of you."

We verbalize it.

"I'm gonna tell you the truth," she says. "The business I'm in . . . the things I do . . . a person is nothing without her word. I'm giving you my word that I'll tell you the whole truth, and you're giving me your word that if I had nothing to do with what happened to him, you'll drop this here and now—my part of this—and not mention it to anyone, including the police."

Blade says, "Give you my word."

"Mine too," I say.

"But is your word any good? Is his? Thing is, all I could get popped for on this is withholding evidence in an investigation, so it's no big deal, but I don't want the cops tramping through my business with their big black boots."

"Our word is good," I say. "Guarantee that. We would've been out of business long ago if it wasn't."

"So here it is. God as my witness. You're right about Aiden coming back here and me taking that part out of the video. Thing is . . . Aiden and I had a little history. Few times over the years . . . if his horny ass couldn't find some little piece to go home with—or in the back alley with—he'd come up here and bang me. He was a pretty good kid. Had a killer body. He'd finish too fast, but he'd be ready to go again pretty soon afterwards. 'Course he'd finish too fast again then, but . . . he'd mostly do what I told him to. Wasn't a regular thing or nothin', but it was fun when it happened. He . . . used to confide in me. I was like a surrogate big sister or somethin'. And when he needed something to help him stay awake to study or whatever, I'd get it for him. That night he was wired and exhausted and just generally fucked up. He called me over there by the bar and said he had seen Jasper, my barback, slip something in a few of the guys' drinks. Said he was watching him because he felt funny and he thought someone had put something in his drink."

"That little prick is who drugged me," Blade says.

"He tried to drug Sammy and got you by mistake," I say.

"I told Aiden to settle down and I'd take care of it," Suzi says.

"Didn't exactly do that, did you?" Blade says. "Two years later and the little creep is still doin' it."

"I'm amending our agreement," I say. "Turn Tollis in and terminate him immediately—something you should've done years ago."

"I'm supposed to care if some privileged, entitled, rape-y fraternity boys get a little dose of their own medicine?"

"Actually, you are," I say. "But I don't have time to teach you how to be a decent human being right now, so just say you'll fire and report him."

"I'll consider it," she says. "Can we get back to that night?

Aiden tried to get belligerent but got dizzy instead and had to sit down. I walked away from it. Don't know what happened after that. Not much, I'm pretty sure. Anyway, when he knocked on my door later, he was really out of it. He wanted to give it a go, but he was in no condition, so I let him lie down on the couch for a while. That's it. I didn't—we didn't have sex or anything. He couldn't."

"Doesn't explain the blood in the back of the hallway," I say.

"Seabass had a nosebleed," she says. "Had nothing to do with Aiden. It looked like Aiden was following him backstage, but he wasn't. Once back here, Aiden came to my office. And Seabass—after doing some crazy shit with his equipment—had one hell of a wicked nosebleed. I'm tellin' you he was already losin' his shit that night. All that business with the equipment . . . I guarantee he thought it had been bugged by the government or some shit like that."

I nod. "Makes sense."

"And I ain't even got no big-time degree or student loans," she says. "Anyway, later that night when he was ready to leave, I let him. I figured he was just going to walk home. Had no idea something would happen to him and it would turn into all this."

"He left from the side door, didn't he?" Blade says.

She nods.

"The camera footage captures the door closing," Blade says. "Doesn't show anything else."

"Yeah," Suzi says. "It shows if someone walks in but not if they walk out, unless they pause in the doorway for some reason."

Blade turns to me. "Sebastian was losing his shit that night and much of what he did with the equipment was strange, but I bet it looks even more bizarre because of what she edited out to hide Aiden's presence back here. And if I'm right about that one shot from the corner store being Aiden . . . it confirms what she's sayin'."

I look back at Suzi. "Is that why you used that door, to hide the fact that he had been back here with you?"

"What? *No.* I wasn't trying to hide him. I hadn't done anything wrong and I couldn't know that something was going to happen to him. It was just bad luck that it happened that way."

"Was this before or after his girlfriend came looking for him?" I ask.

"After. Why?"

"Because that means she could have still been out looking for him when he left."

FIFTY-THREE

BY THE TIME Blade and I get back out into the bar area, the party is breaking up. The band has stopped playing and is tearing down and most of the people have left or are in the process of leaving.

Scanning the room for Amanda and not finding her, we rush down the stairs and out into the parking lot.

The parking lot is busy and full, people in various stages of loading up and pulling out.

The rain has stopped, but every surface is still wet, glistening with refracted light.

Ashlynn bursts out of the front doors and runs over to us.

"The locals news has been covering the Sebastian Lewinsky case," she says. "Someone inside just said they saw me on TV—it's in the background at the hospital when they're reporting on Rick. And your name is in the newspaper in the story about his stabbing. If Dimitri sees either of them. We've got to get Alana and get out of here."

Blade says, "I'll go with her. You see if you can find Amanda. We'll be at Robin's. Meet us there."

They take off and I scan the parking lot again.

A flash of red on the far west end and I am rushing toward Little Red Riding Hood.

"Hey there, Little Red Riding Hood!" I shout.

She doesn't turn or respond in any way.

"Amanda," I yell.

She turns to see me and stops getting into her car.

"What's wrong?" she asks when I reach her. "What is it?"

"Where did you go when you left the bar that night?" I ask.

"That's why you chased me down out here—to ask me that? I went home. I figured he was somewhere with someone and he'd call me the next morning. Why?"

"You didn't see him that night?"

"*What*? NO. Why—what makes you . . . You know I didn't."

"I don't know that," I say. "I didn't even know you were here that night."

"I told you," she says. "I wasn't. Not until after everyone was gone, and then only for a few minutes. And then I drove home."

"You drove all the way here, looked around for a few minutes, and then drove back home? You expect me to believe that?"

"I don't expect you to do anything," she says. "I'm just answering your questions. Why are you asking them?"

"Can anyone verify what time you got home that night?"

"Yeah," she says, nodding, but doesn't offer any more.

"Who?" I ask.

"My roommate. She was a sorter for UPS at the time and was up getting ready for work around that time. I've really got to go. Can you tell me what this is about?"

"As soon as we know, we'll let you know," I say. "We're just trying to exhaust all possibilities."

"Well, I think you've done that where I'm concerned. Definitely exhausted the hell out of me."

CHAPTER
FIFTY-FOUR

I FEEL DOWN AND FRUSTRATED.

I was hoping to find out what happened to Aiden tonight. I thought by getting everyone together in the same place on the same night . . .

Blade took Ashlynn in our car, so I'm walking back.

As I do, I go by every spot where someone was caught on a security camera that night.

Woody walking through the empty streets of an old North Florida port town.

Beneath my boots, the damp pavement shimmers, reflecting the pale illumination of both moon and manmade lights.

The only thing we really found out tonight was a whole lot of who *didn't* do it.

Which could be argued puts us that much closer to knowing who *did* do it, but it feels more like we're back to square one.

Probably the biggest thing we learned or had confirmed tonight is that Aiden got out of the bar and how he did it.

But all that means is he could be anywhere.

I think about how Rick has lived with this for two long years now and how perpetually frustrated he must be. And I hope he'll live to be frustrated by it for many more years to come.

I arrive at the security camera on an automotive parts place at the corner of an intersection about a block from Psycho Suzi's.

Pausing I wonder why he'd come this way.

It's the opposite direction from his home.

If it was him, where was he going? Was he turned around? Confused? Going to meet someone? Or was he avoiding someone? Had he seen Amanda or been told she was there? Was he trying not to be seen by her?

For the rest of the walk back I go over every facet of the case again, questioning everyone's behavior and actions, trying to suss out motivations and the type of poker-like tells that might give away a killer.

They had lived for a decade not knowing what happened to Kaylee. Was this case going to be like that one, slowly going mad because of the not-knowing?

And just like that . . . those two words trigger me—or something in me.

Who is the not knowing not bothering like it should? Whose post-offense behavior indicates both knowledge of the crime and guilt from being involved in it? Who is not acting as they should be? Who is most likely to have done it, now that we know Aiden actually left the bar that night?

"FIGURED I'D FIND YOU HERE," I say.

She turns from Aiden's final resting place and considers me, and I can tell she suspects I finally know.

"It's a lovely grave marker," he says.

She nods.

"Phil killed him, didn't he?" I ask.

She reacts as if having been punched in the stomach, her surprised expression confirming the truth of what I have just said.

She nods, resignation replacing the surprise on her face.

"He didn't mean to," Sheri says. "It was all a horrible accident."

I have found her in her garden on this anniversary of the night of her son's death. She has taken off her costume. She is not a character, but a grieving, broken mother. This is not a holiday but a holy day.

"He never would tell me all the details," she says, "just that Aiden was really strung out and aggressive and they started fussing and then fighting. He didn't mean to kill him. He just tried to survive and subdue him. Aiden's head got bashed in by that damn stone monstrosity of a fireplace I had to have. If I had been here . . . I could've . . . It wouldn't've happened. But you know where I was—a stupid Halloween party out of town. When I got back the next day, Phil had already buried him back here in the garden. Said he didn't want anyone seeing Aiden like that or knowing he had attacked his own father. Was probably more to it than that. I'm sure some self-preservation or panic took over too. What he did was stupid beyond all—but I believed him that it was an accident and he was at least in part trying to protect me from seeing Aiden like that and trying to protect Aiden's reputation. We could've never guessed it would turn into this world-wide unsolved mystery phenomenon, but when it did I couldn't very well reveal what really happened and be able to prevent it from becoming the biggest circus on the planet."

"I'm so sorry for your loss," I say. "For all you've been through—and all that comes with the intense media and true crime community interest."

She nods and thanks me. "How did you figure it out?"

"Just began to apply post-offense behavior to everyone instead of just Sebastian. Thought about how Phil acted both before and after Aiden's disappearance. How you acted toward Phil—while he was alive and since his death. How you've treated this place—how much time and care you lavish on this garden while Phil's generic little headstone is neglected and covered with weeds. The picture of Aiden, the one in the costume he wore that night—the last one he ever took from the day of his death, the one you cropped Phil out of—hanging above that missing chunk of stone on the fireplace. Your unwillingness to sell, your fight with the Estates about your garden and the golf course. How you weren't really afraid of being here in your house because there was no break-in. You staged that yourself. The figure was tall and thin—like you. I remember thinking if it was Aiden, he had lost a lot of weight since he went missing. You hid the costume, which I assume was over your pajamas. You broke the glass out of the backdoor. It's why there was no break-in, just a break-out. At some point later you hid the costume in the sand trap. No one had a motive for doing that, for pretending to be Aiden and telling you he's okay, except you. But I'm still not sure why you did it."

"Me either," she says. "It was so stupid. I didn't think it through. Just thought it would throw some confusion into the mix, maybe get some people to thinking he was still alive, so they wouldn't look too closely at me and Phil. It was . . . just a dumb, dumb thing I did."

"Did you post the message from Aiden on Phil's memorial guestbook?"

She nods. "Another moment of brilliance on my part," she says, shaking her head and letting out a harsh little laugh. "Did some research online on how to do it. Put on a disguise and went to an internet cafe and . . . So stupid. What else gave me away?"

"How at peace you've been with supposedly not knowing what really happened to Aiden. Not knowing what happened to Aiden is disturbing me and Blade far more than you—and the only way that can be is that you don't not-know. You know. You were absolutely fine with us stopping the investigation once Serge threatened us. You were fine because you already knew. You had been humoring us throughout because you already knew what really happened. Phil killed Aiden. And you killed Phil."

"Well, I guess I did, but not really," she says. "I was so . . . livid. I believed him. I knew how Aiden could get when he was on drugs and alcohol after a week of no sleep, but . . . I just couldn't forgive him—even for an accident. Couldn't let it go. It just festered inside of me, grew into this huge black thing eating my insides out. We were in the attic getting the Christmas decorations down—something I did not feel like or want to be doing —and I just lost it. All I did was charge him and shove him. That's it. He fell backwards, tripped on one of the exposed trusses and fell through the ceiling onto the floor in the hallway. It knocked the breath out of him but he seemed fine. Not that I cared. I didn't. He went to the hospital to get checked out and when they asked what happened he just told them he stumbled and fell through. When he came home he acted like nothing had happened. Didn't even mention it. And neither did I. I knew I owed him an apology, but I just couldn't . . . Three days later, he was dead. Delayed aortic dissection. They say the trauma from the fall caused a small, pain-free tear in his aorta. They probably would've seen it if they had done an MRI, but when the chest X-ray was normal they didn't do anything else. So, yes, I guess I killed him—at least the action I took led to his death, but when I lost it and shoved him it wasn't with the intention of killing him. Who would ever think shoving someone would kill them?"

"Does anyone else know?" I ask.

She shakes her head. "Only two people on the planet know—and we're both here right now."

I nod and think about that, and we are quiet a few moments.

"What are you going to do?" she asks.

"What do you mean?"

"Now that you know," she says.

"Oh," I say. "Nothing."

"You're not going to tell anyone?"

I shake my head. "There's only two people I want to tell—just for their sake. Rick and Blade. I know I can't tell Rick because of the position it would put him in and what he'd have to do about it. But Blade . . . will keep our secret."

"Thank you for your understanding and kindness. And for calling it *our secret.*"

I start to say something but stop as the barrel of a handgun is pressed into the back of my head.

SHERI'S EYES grow wide as alarm feels her face and her mouth falls open.

"Hate to interrupt such a tender moment," a voice behind me says.

I start to turn to see who's speaking, but the gun is jammed deeper into the back of my head and the voice says, "Keep facing straight ahead at the old lady. And, old lady, don't look at me."

Sheri averts her gaze.

"Who sent you?" I ask.

"Does it matter?" he asks. "Dead is dead. Doesn't matter who pays the piper."

His accent is American Northeast, not Russian.

"Serge or Dimitri?" I ask.

"Not that it matters but don't know no Serge. What is he? A fashion designer?"

I laugh. "Yeah," I say, "I complained about the cut of my suit and he vowed revenge."

"Bet you don't even own a suit," he says. "And you've never owned anything tailored in your life. Where is the black bitch who likes to cut people?"

"Oh, I'm sure she'll be coming up behind you and slicing you open any minute now."

"I hope she tries. I sincerely do."

"Why would Dimitri send hired help?" I say. "I thought this was personal for him."

"I kill you I get one fee," he says. "I deliver you to him I get a much larger fee. Where are the others? I'm short a nigger, a stripper, and a rugrat."

"No way we're givin' them up," I say.

"I start torturing you or the old lady you might feel differently."

"As you say," Sheri says. "I'm old. Don't mind dying. Hell, I'm lookin' forward to aspects of it. You won't get anyone's whereabouts out of me."

"We'll see."

Since he never told me to raise my hands, I've kept them down at my sides, and my right one is near the old west replica sixshooter.

I keep trying to figure my best move. Should I grab it and fire behind me, hoping I can get a round into him before he blows the back of my skull off? Should I wait and hope for a distraction or at least until I'm facing him?

The fact that he hasn't removed my gun or asked me to do it means he must think it's just a prop.

Is he alone or are others with him? We've only heard his voice but I'd be surprised if he's by himself. Even if I am able to grab my gun and fire a round blindly into him, there could be someone else back there to take out me and Sheri in the process.

I catch Sheri's eye and glance down at my gun.

"House is empty," a different voice says, as footfalls approach.

"Where are they?" the voice directly behind me asks.

"Who?"

He hits me on the back of the head with the butt of his gun, and though the blow isn't much, I act as though it is, and take the opportunity to fall to the ground.

Hunched over and hiding what I'm doing, I remove my weapon and hold it beneath me.

"Get up," he says. "I barely touched you, you little pussy. This is gonna be even easier than I—"

I spin around on the ground, come up with the gun, and shoot him in the chest, a bloom of blood spreading across his shirt, looking black in the moonlight.

Before I can fire at the other guy or he can fire at me, a flap of his scalp flops forward and a slice of his skull blows off.

As he crumples to the ground, Bobby Doll is revealed coming up behind him.

I nod my appreciation and admiration to him, my ears still ringing from the shots, then turn to make sure Sheri is okay.

She's in shock, but unhurt.

"Nice move, cowboy," Bobby Doll says.

"You too. When'd you get here?"

"Few minutes ago. Was tryin' to figure out how to take them both out without them shootin' you two and then all of a sudden Sheriff Woody changed the equation. Let's get them out of here before some neighbor decides to investigate what sounded like backfire in the backyard."

"Or . . ." Sheri says, "these could be the two who broke into my house last week."

Doll looks at me. "Your call. I can make them disappear or you can give me your gun and I can be the one who shot 'em."

"I was thinkin' Robin and I shot them," she says. "Two old ladies sitting in my garden eating trick-or-treat candy when two hoodlums came up and accosted us. But we were ready."

"Hoodlums," Doll says. "I like it."

Sheri says, "No one's going to question two old ladies. We'll be heroines. And nobody will fuck with me about my garden ever again."

Doll says, "My heater's not traceable. Yours?"

"It actually belonged to Phil, Sheri's husband," I say.

"Perfect. Lot less work for me if we go with her plan. Let the cops deal with the bodies. Plus it's more embarrassing for Dimitri. But it's your call."

"*SHEE-IT,*" Blade says. "Sheri's got a fuckin' side hustle covering up murders."

"Ah, actually," I say, "accidental and self-defense deaths."

In the end we decided to go with Sheri's plan, and now she and Robin are local legends. And the two men they killed, Jamison Elliot and Miles Turner, are suspected to have been involved in Aiden's disappearance.

"So touchy," she says. "*Shee-it*, okay, self-defense."

It's a few days later, and we have just returned from the hospital after visiting Rick, who, though he has a lot of healing and rehab in front of him, is going to make it, and may even be back at work before Christmas.

"You think what Suzi said about Sebastian could be true? He did all that shit with the equipment 'cause his ass was having a psychotic break?"

I nod. "I've heard of shit like that before. A person's paranoia has them believing possessions of theirs are wired by the government to spy on them—refrigerators, receptacles, blow-dryers. I know a guy who showed up at his ex-girlfriend's apartment with his car headlamp convinced the government was watching him through it."

"Why you think Serge warned us off if they didn't have anything to do with Aiden's disappearance?"

"Well, they did have *something* to do with it—and he may have thought Suzi had more to do with it than she did, but I suspect it's because of all their other criminal activities. Who knows what motivates a man like him?"

"When you went to get Rick's snacks, he told me they arrested Jasper Tollis this morning."

"Way overdue."

"Why you think Suzi let him keep workin' there after she found out what he was doin'?"

"Leverage," I say. "Probably blackmailed him into doin' all sort of shit for her."

"I'm tempted to burn that place to the ground before we leave town."

"Tollis will turn state's evidence on them. Their days are numbered. Rick'll see to it when he gets back."

"Then I think our work here is done," she says. "Let's get your ass back home before you violate your probation anymore.

"THAT'LL BE TWO DOLLARS, SIR," Alana is saying.

She has just made me a pretend cup of coffee.

We are in Oaks by the Bay park, playing beneath an enormous old oak tree in the late afternoon of a pleasant and picturesque North Florida November day.

I pay her with pretend money and take my cup of coffee.

"Thanks, bruh," she says. "Come again to see us."

She's heard someone—most likely on a TV show—call someone *bruh*, and she's been using it a lot, saying it with perfect attitude and diction. She got her version of *come back to see us* from me when our roles were reversed and I was the barista.

"Have a good day," I say.

"Have a good day, bruh," she says.

"Thanks, bruh," I say.

"No, I'm a sister."

"Oh, sorry. Have a good day, my sister."

Ashlynn had decided to come back home with us. She and Alana are living with me, and Blade, Bobby Doll, Pistol Pete, Clyde Broussard, and Lexi Miller are helping me provide round the clock protection for them. In fact, Doll, wearing a trench coat with a rifle beneath and looking like a streaker, is leaning against a pine tree less than fifteen feet away.

An elderly couple from the neighborhood strolls by, waves, and says, "Hey, Alana."

"They just *hey*ed me," she says.

"They sure did."

"How'd they know my name?"

"They're our neighbors. And everyone around here adores you. But no one more than me. I love you so much and am so glad you're home. I missed you sooo bad."

As if not hearing any of that, she says, "Okay, you be the coffee person now and I'll be the . . ."

"Customer," I say.

"Yeah."

"Okay," I say. "Hi, ma'am, welcome to Uncle Luc's Grind House. What can I get started for you?"

"I would like a coffee please, sir," she says. "Thanks, bruh."

"You got it."

As she's drinking her pretend coffee, Lexi walks up.

"I'm so glad to have you guys back," she says. "Missed you so much."

"Everybody missed me," Alana says. "Would you like some coffee, Lexi?"

"I'd love some."

"Okay," she says. "I will fix you a cup."

She takes the cup and maker from me and begins to earnestly prepare her a fresh cup.

"Can I take you two to lunch?" she asks.

I look up at her, squinting in the low afternoon sunlight behind her, and in that moment I realize just how much I've missed her, how much I've missed my home, and how with Ashlynn and Alana back it was home once again.

"*We'll* take *you* with all the profits from our coffee shop."

She laughs, then we are quiet a moment, listening to Alana talk to herself as she makes the coffee.

"Guess what I heard this morning?" she says. "Looks like those two shooters have been linked to Dimitri and he's being looked at in connection with Aiden Shaw's disappearance. They say there's a good chance he'll run back to Russia."

I nod. "Nice—unless it makes him more desperate. Even if or especially if he leaves he may decide to take a run at us before he goes."

"It's always something, isn't it?" she says. "It never stops. They just keep coming."

"That's true of life and everyone's work," I say. "Ours just happens to involve playing for blood."

"Hey, sister," Alana says to Lexi, "your coffee's ready, ma'am."

"Thank you, ma'am."

"That'll be ten dollars," Alana says, holding out her little hand.

"Coffee's gone up," I say.

"Still a bargain," Lexi says, pulling actual money from her pocket and giving it to Alana.

"*Oh, wow,*" she exclaims as she takes the real dollar bills. "I'm rich."

Lexi looks at me and says, "Yes you are. You truly are. Far beyond what you will ever know."

SERIES SALE

For a limited time the entire John Jordan series is on sale!

CLICK HERE to complete your series for the best price EVER!

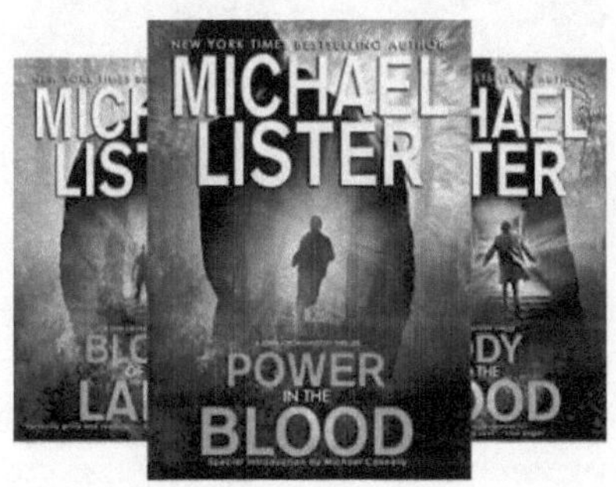

JIMMY RILEY NOIR SERIES

A VULNERABLE YOUNG woman being followed. A PI determined to protect her. Former lovers embroiled in an intense mystery thriller fraught with intrigue and danger. A sexy, romantic, suspenseful ride through the atmospheric 1940s for fans of film noir and the classic hard-boiled detective novel.

Someone is following Lauren Lewis.

She ducks into the office of PI, Jimmy "Soldier" Riley, not to hire him, but to find out if he's the one following her. Back when they were lovers he told her if he ever decided to, she'd never know he was there.

It's1940's Panama City, Florida. The world is at war, and the growing panhandle paradise is doing its part. Tyndall Field is training pilots. Wainwright Shipyard is building battleships. The Naval Section Base is protecting vessels in the Gulf. The Dixie Sherman Hotel is hosting celebrities such as Clark Gable. Harry Lewis, a wealthy banker, is running for mayor, unaware his wife is running for her life.

With a secret to hide and a husband running for mayor in a city exploding and expanding like no other time in history, Lauren doesn't want trouble, but she's about to get a double-barrel full of it. Only one man can help her, and though it might destroy him, he doesn't mind. Better to die than be the walking wounded.

Get The Big Goodbye and begin your fun, romantic, and mysterious journey with Jimmy and Lauren today!

"Lister's hard-edged prose ranks with the best of contemporary noir fiction." *Publisher's Weekly* **Starred Review**

ABOUT THE AUTHOR

New York Times bestselling and award-winning novelist Michael Lister is a native Floridian best known for his acclaimed John Jordan "Blood" mystery thriller series.

Michael grew up in north Florida near the Gulf of Mexico and the Apalachicola River in a small town world famous for tupelo honey.

Captivated by story since childhood, Michael has a love for language and narrative inspired by the Southern storytelling tradition.

Before becoming a full-time novelist in 2000, Michael taught high school, worked as a college professor and inspirational speaker, owned and operated a bookstore, wrote a popular syndicated column, served as a newspaper editor, operated a community theater, wrote plays and screenplays, and worked for a production company. He has lectured extensively in the areas of creative writing, film, literature, spirituality, and self-help.

In the 90s, Michael was the youngest chaplain within the Florida Department of Corrections. For nearly a decade, he served as a contract, staff, then senior chaplain at three different facilities in the Panhandle of Florida—a singular experience that led to his first novel, 1997's critically acclaimed, **POWER IN THE BLOOD**.

Michael is also the author of the Burke and Blade Panama City Beach PI series (**THE NIGHT OF, etc.**), the 1940s Jimmy Riley noir series (**THE BIG GOODBYE, etc.**), and the thrillers **DOUBLE EXPOSURE, BURNT OFFERINGS,** and **SEPARATION ANXIETY.**

Michael is the recipient of two Florida Book Awards—for **DOUBLE EXPOSURE** and **BLOOD SACRIFICE**, respectively. His work has spent time on both the *New York Times* and the *USA Today* Bestseller lists, been translated into German, and adapted into stage plays. Currently, **DOUBLE EXPOSURE** is in development for a feature film and the John Jordan books for a TV series.

Michael lives in North Florida with his wife Denise, where in between writing stints, he enjoys time with his family and friends, playing basketball, and making music.

ALSO BY MICHAEL LISTER

(John Jordan Novels)

Power in the Blood

Blood of the Lamb

The Body and the Blood

Double Exposure

Blood Sacrifice

Rivers to Blood

Burnt Offerings

Innocent Blood

(Special Introduction by Michael Connelly)

Separation Anxiety

Blood Money

Blood Moon

Thunder Beach

Blood Cries

A Certain Retribution

Blood Oath

Blood Work

Cold Blood

Blood Betrayal

Blood Shot

Blood Ties

Blood Stone

Blood Trail

Bloodshed

Blue Blood

And the Sea Became Blood

The Blood-Dimmed Tide

Blood and Sand

A John Jordan Christmas

Blood Lure

Blood Pathogen

Beneath a Blood-Red Sky

Out for Blood

What Child is This?

Blood Reckoning

(Burke and Blade Mystery Thrillers)

The Night Of

The Night in Question

All Night Long

(Jimmy Riley Novels)

The Girl Who Said Goodbye

The Girl in the Grave

The Girl at the End of the Long Dark Night

The Girl Who Cried Blood Tears

The Girl Who Blew Up the World

(Merrick McKnight / Reggie Summers Novels)

Thunder Beach

A Certain Retribution

Blood Oath

Blood Shot

(Remington James Novels)

Double Exposure

(includes intro by Michael Connelly)

Separation Anxiety

Blood Shot

(Sam Michaels / Daniel Davis Novels)

Burnt Offerings

Blood Oath

Cold Blood

Blood Shot

(Love Stories)

Carrie's Gift

(Short Story Collections)

North Florida Noir

Florida Heat Wave

Delta Blues

Another Quiet Night in Desperation

(The Meaning Series)

Meaning Every Moment

The Meaning of Life in Movies

Sign up for Michael's newsletter by clicking here or go to
www.MichaelLister.com and receive a free book.